D1063207

Saving Jasey

Diane Tullson

ORCA BOOK PUBLISHERS

National Library of Canada Cataloguing in Publication Data
Tullson, Diane, 1958-
Saving Jasey

ISBN 1-55143-220-X

I. Title.
PS8589.U6055S28   jC813'.6   C2001-910947-4   PZ7.T844Sa 2001

First published in the United States, 2002

Library of Congress Catalog Card Number: 2001092679

Orca Book Publishers gratefully acknowledges the support for
our publishing programs provided by the following agencies:
The Government of Canada through the Book Publishing Industry
Development Program (BPIDP), The Canada Council
for the Arts, and the British Columbia Arts Council.

Cover design: Christine Toller
Cover photograph: Stone/Chris Thomaidis
Printed and bound in Canada

IN CANADA: IN THE UNITED STATES:
Orca Book Publishers   Orca Book Publishers
PO Box 5626, Station B   PO Box 468
Victoria, BC Canada   Custer, WA   USA
V8R 6S4   98240-0468

03 02   • 5 4 3 2

For Mom, with love.
Then, now, always.

Acknowledgement:

Thanks to the writers of Deep Cove, Delta and
Surrey: a communal heart and mind.

ONE

[1]

Dad had his handgun apart, the pieces set carefully on a clean white cloth on the kitchen table. He squirted oil onto a rag and rubbed the gray metal of the barrel. At work he carries the gun in a black holster under his jacket.

I don't know if he's ever had to use it. Mostly he just drives around in a little car checking that gates are closed and doors are locked. But he'd probably like to.

"Old man Murphy is thinking of putting dogs on site." He polished the gun barrel to a soft gleam. I was sitting across from him, doing my math homework. Mr. Murphy is my dad's boss. I'm pretty sure he doesn't know Dad carries the gun.

"Says they'll cut costs. Just have to feed them." He shook his head. "And not too much, either, Murphy says, because they're meaner when they're a little hungry." He paused to dig in his ear. "Fat lot of good

1

is a dog after a lump of poisoned meat goes over the fence. Bye-bye, Fido."

I couldn't tell if Dad was talking about a thief throwing the meat over, or him doing it. The finger came out of his ear with a pop.

"He's an idiot, old man Murphy. If he thinks an animal can do what we do, then he should haul his fat butt out of bed and park it in a cold Toyota for eight hours at a stretch. See what it's like."

I packed up my books to go upstairs. This was starting to take a familiar turn.

"Where do you think you're going, boy?" He jabbed the oily rag in my face.

"Just up to my room. I've got tons of homework."

"Sit where you were. Keep your old man company."

I sat back down.

"The thing about dogs is they're unpredictable. Sure they guard. You wouldn't catch me on the wrong side of a fence with a Rottie or shepherd. Uh-uh." He clicked the chamber and barrel together. "Or Dobermans. They're the worst. Just teeth and no brains."

Kind of like you, I thought, only without the teeth.

I got up to go. His face hardened to a scowl. "Sit down, I told you." His eyes drilled into me. "It's not like you have anything real pressing to do. Not like you have a life."

He worked a clean rag in behind the trigger. "The

thing with guard dogs is they've been beaten. Makes them crazy. You got to do it; otherwise they're no better than pets. But they'll eat one another, just for something to do." He sighted down the barrel. "Saw a Doberman get into a nest of kittens once. It wasn't pretty."

I looked over to Tiger, my cat, on the back of the couch. Cover your ears, Tiger.

"Now a regular dog, he'd just gobble them up. Crunch. Crunch. Crunch. But a bad dog, he'll make it last. Unholy noise, those kittens made." He smiled when he said that. "Get me a Pepsi."

He was working tonight so he stayed away from the beer. I got up and went to the fridge.

"The mother cat, she lit into the dog for all she was worth. Not that it was much against a Doberman. Right to the death."

I set down the Pepsi in front of him.

"What do you think, I can open it with my teeth? Open it for me." He shook his head like I was an idiot. "That's the thing with animals. No matter how bad it is, they suffer it out to the end. Like them wildebeest on *Wild Kingdom*, and the pack of hyenas chowing down on them while they're still alive. Sit, I'm telling you!"

I sighed, flopped into my chair, and rested my head on my hand. It was almost 10:00. He'd have to go sooner or later.

"Humans are the only creatures to kill themselves. They're weak, can't stand too much pain. Oh, some people think whales kill themselves when they get beached, but they're idiots. Only people commit suicide." He tapped an oily finger on the side of his head. Big thick fingers on a big thick man.

"Of course, you don't get life insurance if you kill yourself. Say this gun went off, spattered my brains over your mother's cupboards. 'It was an accident,' you'd say, whining like you do so well. The insurance money would let you live like a king. But if I off myself, then too bad. They don't pay."

If I got up early, I could finish my math before school. Roger had done a couple of questions with me so I'd know how to answer them.

"Insurance companies get rich off sick bastards that kill themselves. 'Sorry ma'am, we know you've been paying the premiums for a gazillion years, but your husband jumped off a bridge. You'll just have to get yourself a job.'"

No way I could get the reading done tonight. My eyes felt like lead. Maybe Trist would tell me what happened in the chapter.

" 'And the kiddies, why, they'll have to work at McDonald's for the rest of their lives, because they won't get any money from us for school.'"

I had Social Studies too, but that was just labeling

a map. I could do it when I got to school. Dad slipped the gun into its holster and stood up. Finally. He was going to work.

"That's the thing, Gavin. You're lucky you have me to take care of this family." He snapped his pressed shirt off the back of the chair, put it on, and buttoned it. The crest on the sleeve read "Secure-Watch." Dad works permanent night shift. Home at eight, sleeps until five, gets up, eats, watches TV, and goes to work. On his days off he keeps the same schedule. "It's hard on your system to change shifts." Instead of going to work he goes to the bar.

"Not like school is in your plans, anyway." He stretched his chin forward to do up the top button. "Not in a million years." He tucked the shirt in and did up his pants. His belly bulged over the belt. "You'll be real happy to work at McDonald's."

He took the gun out, loaded the shells, then replaced it in the holster and strapped it on. He drained the Pepsi, the bump in his throat riding up and down under his collar with each greedy swallow. With a belch he tossed the empty can on the table, took a tie out of the pocket of his shirt and clipped it on.

"Clean up this stuff, why don't you." He jerked his thumb at the rags and oil, the Pepsi can. My father, the crime fighter, was finally going to work.

Two

The gate into Trist's backyard clicked closed behind me. His grandfather was stooped over the deck, paint-spattered overalls criss-crossing his back, a block of sandpaper held poised in his hand.

"Morning, Grandpa Jack."

Everyone calls him Grandpa Jack.

"Gavin. Watch you don't lean your bike where I've been painting." He gestured with a sweeping thumb at the fence, deck, and house. "It's just here and there. Touch-ups, you know."

Like I would. Our house up the street has worn the same paint the builders put on, and it has scales like a fish where the sun hits. I set my bike on its kickstand and picked my way to the back door. Grandpa Jack bent to sand a tiny pockmark from the deck.

They're all McVeighs in this house: Trist, his mother, grandfather, grandmother, and Great Uncle

6

Pat too, although he's in a home now. And Trist's sister, Jasey. Jasey McVeigh.

"Are you going in or letting the flies in first?" He said it with a smile.

"Uh, yeah." I pulled the door closed, a flush creeping from my neck to my cheeks to the roots of my red hair. Through the screen, Grandpa Jack was shaking his head.

I've been friends with Trist since he moved in here when we were six. Now we're in eighth grade, the first week of it, the year stretching before us dry and colorless like sand. I slid onto a kitchen chair, Jasey's, and rested my elbows on the damp spot where Gran had wiped up breakfast crumbs.

"Hello, Gavin." Gran smiled as she filled brown lunch bags. She wore a golf shirt and shorts, and her silver hair was swept into a clasp at the nape of her neck. Her legs were brown and strong. "Trist!" she trumpeted up the stairs. "Don't make yourself late!"

I traced my finger on the wooden surface of the table, imagining Jasey's hands resting here, imagining my hands covering hers, imagining their smoothness.

Imagining. Last week I was sitting on Trist's couch with him and his sister Jasey, eating a big bowl of popcorn and watching some movie about Africa. A popcorn kernel lodged in my throat, and I started to cough.

"Take a sip of your pop." Jasey leaned toward me, concerned, her leg suddenly against mine.

Between coughs I managed to gasp, "It's all gone."

"He's choking to death, Trist. Give him a sip of yours!" Her leg was warm. Really warm.

Through my streaming eyes, I saw Trist look at his sister, then shake his head. "He'll get chunks in it."

With an exasperated sound directed at Trist, Jasey pressed her can into my hand. It was root beer, the same kind I had already finished. I lifted it to my mouth, conscious of the wetness her lips had left on the can, conscious of her beside me, her soap smell and silk hair and how I wanted to weld her leg there, right next to mine. I set my lips on the can where hers had been, the burning in my throat replaced by the burning of my cheeks, the sweetness of the root beer lost in the rush of blood, the popcorn kernel long gone. With greedy gulps, I drained the root beer.

I handed her the empty can. She shook it, her eyebrows lifting a bit. "Are you all right now?"

I nodded.

Her voice was quiet, like it was just for me. "No chunks. See?" She tipped the pop can to her mouth with her lips parted slightly, her eyes half closed, holding it there to capture the few remaining drops. My tongue became a rolled-up sock. She swallowed, the smooth white skin on her throat barely moving. Then she lowered the can and smiled at me.

"I'm glad you're all right." She shifted toward

me, and for an endless instant I thought she was going to kiss me. Then she put her hand on my head and tousled my hair. "You're far too young to die."

"She's not here." With a jolt, I realized Trist had appeared at the counter, stuffing his lunch into his pack, a banana disappearing into his face. Mine flooded, again.

Trist grinned, his cheeks bulging with banana. He pushed hair out of his eyes—brown hair tinged gold from the summer, blue eyes, like Jasey's—and shouldered his pack.

"Left hours ago. Did you finish the reading assignment for Ms. Beastly?"

Gran eyed the wall clock and shooed us to the door. Trist ducked from her kiss, but I let her plant one on me. She wiped a trace of lipstick off my cheek. "Be brilliant today. If I'm not here when you get home, make yourselves a snack. We're doing eighteen holes and then going to see Pat."

The morning held the promise of blue sky and sunshine. As I pushed my bike back through the gate I wished I could stay there at the McVeigh place, where nothing ever went wrong.

"You didn't do the reading, did you?"

I shrugged. "I can do it during music-listening."

Trist swung his leg over his bike and pushed off down the lane. "Your brother giving you a hard time?"

My brother Blake. Blake the Flake. Black Blake.

9

Fifteen and poison. In the same class as Jasey, even though he managed to fail most of his courses last term.

"No. I just fell asleep."

"If you can keep up to me, I'll tell you what you missed." He stood on his pedals, long legs pumping, and the bike shot ahead.

I curled over my handlebars and forced oxygen to my stubby legs. The pedals caught the energy, feeding it to the chain, to the hungry tires. It's a better bike than Trist's, better than I should own. I got it as a demo. I shoveled snow and cut grass all last year to save up for this bike. It's silver-gray, with titanium forks, and geared to take hills on the wings of an angel. I pulled even with Trist.

"What's she wearing today?"

"Green plaid. Or something orange and stretchy."

I nosed past him. My shirt was stuck to my back and my hair plastered with sweat. "Not Ms. Beastly. Your sister."

"Oh. Her. She left before I got up. Went running, or something."

Yes. Running. Like one of those gazelles you see on nature shows with their graceful bent legs. I sat back a bit on the seat, the image of Jasey in running tights causing spots to lift in front of my eyes. Trist shot in front.

We locked our bikes and walked into class. "You'll like this book," he said. "It's about a kid who survives in the wild all on his own. I read ahead."

I knew what the book was about. Mrs. Montgomery, the learning assistant, had told me about it when she'd given it to me at the end of last year so I could start on it over the summer. It had collected dust on my windowsill.

Which was a mistake.

"Gavin, you'll see me after school." Ms. Priestly stapled me to my seat with her eyes. "Vanessa, would YOU like to tell us please how the protagonist found himself alone in the woods."

Trist met my gaze and rolled his eyes. I wasn't sure if it was because I hadn't done the reading, or because now we'd hear the very long Vanessa version of the story. She was standing up to better address the class, her golden curls bouncing on her shoulders. I slumped in my seat. With my best pencil I sketched a dragon on the cover of my English notebook—curved fangs, spiked tail, and if I could have drawn it, the fetid breath of decaying flesh.

Ms. Priestly was mercifully brief.

"Gavin, you have it in you to do better than this. It's the third time in as many days that you haven't attended to your homework." She set herself into her chair. Ms. Priestly had taught my brother Blake; maybe she even taught my folks. She wore white orthopedic shoes and knee-high hose under huge skirts of indescribable patterns. Her hair was bright yellow, combed in fat yellow worms off her pink forehead. I looked down at my shoes. In the toe of one I could see my gray sock.

"I will do all I can for you this year." She folded her spotted hands in her lap. "What will you do for yourself?"

I looked up, then back down. She didn't seem to require an answer.

"What's Blake up to these days?"

I allowed myself a breath, and lifted my head. She was looking at me with eyes that seemed to know what I was thinking.

What should I tell her? Mom says that Blake is going through a phase. "Stand by your brother," Mom says. "This isn't easy for him."

Yeah, well, it's a real cakewalk for me. Makes me wish I were switched at birth. That my real family has a set of dishes where half of it hasn't been broken in someone's fury. Where you can have a friend over. Where you can own one single thing without it becoming someone else's. Just like that.

Blake says stuff to my mom that makes her cry,

just because he can. Sometimes I stand in the other room listening, not because I want to, but because I figure that somehow my being there stops him from doing anything worse. If I ever pray, that's when I do it.

"He's okay. Repeating some courses, you know."

Ms. Priestly leaned forward, her eyes like lasers. "You'll keep up with this class." She sat back in the chair. "Unless, of course, you want to become just like your brother."

THREE

"Monopoly tonight?" I crushed the yogurt container and licked the pink goo from the heel of my hand. It was Friday, and every Friday night at the McVeighs' we play Monopoly.

Trist poked a tuna sandwich into his bulging cheeks. His eyes bugged out with the load and his nostrils flared to get enough air.

"You're going to die eating like that."

He swallowed, chewed, and swallowed again. The remaining mass he moved into one cheek, then he drew half his chocolate milk up through the straw and down his throat. I watched chunks of tuna trail back down the straw.

"Seven bells. Prepare to be whooped." He crumpled his lunch bag and tossed a good cross-cafeteria shot at the garbage can.

I showered after supper and combed my hair down

14

hard so that it wouldn't dry funny. I put two coats of stink-nice under my arms and pulled on a clean T-shirt. The sleeves were sharply creased. Mom irons everything. I found socks with no holes and belted my jeans. In the kitchen, I kissed Mom on the cheek.

"You look nice. You going out?" She tightened the belt on her robe and brushed a fleck of lint off my shoulder.

"McVeighs'. For Monopoly. It's Friday."

She glanced outside, as if that might tell her the day of the week. "Oh, sure it is." The lines deepened on her forehead.

"I'll be back around eleven."

"Uh-huh." She chewed on a thumbnail. I knew that look. She was thinking about Blake. He hadn't come home after school, maybe wouldn't make it home tonight. Or he'd come crashing in at dawn, stinking of smoke and beer, one shoe missing, puking on the step. He'd sleep around the clock, then get up looking for blood like most people look for breakfast. My blood. Or my mother's.

"Say good-bye to your father."

"I already did." I pushed through the screen door, the sense of freedom making me giddy. I walked to Trist's nice and easy, so as not to get all sweaty. His mom let me in.

"Jelly donut or fritter?"

15

"Jelly." I reached into the donut box and made my selection. There were all kinds of donuts. Mrs. McVeigh picks up a box every Friday night on her way home from her job at the bank. But I always choose either a jelly or a fritter. I took my spot at the table.

"Those things are like eating a mouse." Grandpa Jack was already at the table, a plain glazed in front of him. "The dusty sugar is just like fur. Then you bite in and the red stuff oozes out, like entrails."

I severed the donut in one bite and let the raspberry filling hang for a second before catching it with my tongue. Grandpa Jack shuddered in mock disgust.

Trist and Gran slid in on one side of the table, armed with double chocolate and maple glazed. I swallowed the last of the donut and licked the corners of my mouth clean.

"You got white stuff on your nose," said Trist.

I wiped it quickly with the back of my hand.

Mrs. McVeigh set out the board and started sorting the cash. She was banker. It only made sense.

"Aren't we going to wait for Jasey?" I said.

Trist spoke around a mouthful of donut. "She's going out."

"But it's Friday night!" The squeak in my voice appalled me.

I caught Mrs. McVeigh and Gran exchanging

looks. Trist shrugged. "That means I can be the shoe."
He reached for Jasey's playing piece.

"NO! Nobody should use Jasey's shoe. If she's
not playing, it should be retired!"

Grandpa Jack rolled his eyes and reached for the
little car. "We don't get playing, then I'll miss the
10:00 news."

Jasey's perfume came through the kitchen before
she did. Trist wrinkled his nose, but I took it in until
my head felt light.

Trist's mother couldn't keep the panic out of her
voice. "You're not leaving the house dressed like that."

I willed my mouth to close. Jasey stalked through
the kitchen, her jeans slung low on her hips, a tiny
cropped T-shirt flaring where her breasts lifted it from
her body. A small snort escaped from Grandpa Jack.

Jasey ignored her mother.

"You're at least going to wear a jacket!"

Jasey flipped her dark curls over one shoulder, a
look of irritation crossing her brows, then indiffer-
ence. "I don't need one."

I glanced at Trist, but he was overly busy shuf-
fling the Chance cards. Grandpa Jack was studying
his hands. Grandma was watching Trist's mother. It
was all I could do not to stare at Jasey. There was
more of her showing than I'd ever seen.

She leaned over the table, brushing her lips first

over Grandpa Jack's cheek, then her mother's. "See you at eleven."

Her mother set her hand over Jasey's arm. "I mean it, Jasey. I don't want you wearing that outfit. What about one of those nice things we got you for school? That white turtleneck?"

Jasey snapped her arm free, her eyes flashing. "This is fine, Mother. I can dress myself."

"Then why haven't you?"

Jasey sucked in an exasperated sigh. "I like what I'm wearing. My friends like what I wear. Keep out of it."

"Young lady …"

"I'm late."

"Well, you won't be wearing that when we visit Uncle Pat tomorrow!"

"I won't be going!" And with that Jasey spun out of the kitchen, the back door flying closed behind her.

The bareness of her belly was still making my eyes hurt. Grandpa Jack cleared his throat. Grandma took the dice from the box. "Let's roll to see who goes first."

Trist's mother sat watching the door, bright spots of color on her cheeks. Speaking quietly, almost to herself, she said, "She's never given me any cause to worry. Never any trouble, Jasey." With a shake of her head she turned back to the table. "Yes. Let's roll."

Mrs. McVeigh is clearly Jasey's mother. Their hair curls in the same thick dark loops. Jasey wears hers a little longer; Mrs. McVeigh contains hers a little more. They have the same rosewater skin, and tiny noses with the smallest tilt. Mrs. McVeigh has brown eyes. Jasey's are blue. It would be bad form to admire your friend's mother, and Mrs. McVeigh is almost like my own mother, and I only draw the comparison between her and Jasey to illustrate my point. Mrs. McVeigh is beautiful.

Grandpa Jack cornered the board with Park Place and Boardwalk. It's a rare Friday night when he doesn't.

"Allies." Trist poked his orange cards at my railroads. I surveyed the table. Mrs. McVeigh had already allied with Gran and they had both purple sides of the board all sewn up.

"You're on." I didn't stand a chance without him.

Mrs. McVeigh brought Monopoly to Friday nights. She's widowed. She and Trist and Jasey moved in when it happened. When we first started playing, Trist and I were so small we couldn't read the Chance cards. Uncle Pat still lived at the house then, and Gran would wheel him into the kitchen so he could feel a part of the fun. He's a big man, just like Grandpa Jack, but really thin. He used to comb his hair the same way as his brother, although now that I'm thinking about it, maybe Grandpa Jack combed his hair, and that's why it was the same. He lurched in his chair, his hands curled in his lap, his chin jerking back and forth. I couldn't understand him, but Gran and Grandpa Jack pretty much knew what he was saying.

"No, it's not Sam," they'd say, gesturing to Trist. "It's his boy, Tristan. Sam's passed away now."

Uncle Pat would lurch forward. He'd ask the same question over and over. When I first knew him, I thought he was being rude. Then I understood that he just didn't remember asking the question.

"It's Trist. Sam's boy. Sam's gone, Pat."

Uncle Pat lives in a nursing home now. It was too hard for Gran and Grandpa Jack to take care of him. He was having trouble swallowing and he was getting too thin. Grandpa Jack cried when they moved him to the home.

Trist's great-grandfather had the disease, and his great-great grandmother, and as far back as anyone knows, someone in this family has had it.

Trist and I came close to winning, but Grandpa Jack wiped us out on Boardwalk with three hotels. I didn't mind losing, with Jasey's chair sitting empty all evening. Trist stretched his feet out onto it and I knocked them off.

"Grandpa Jack, you take the prize for tonight." Mrs. McVeigh handed him the last donut.

"And not a moment too soon." He glanced at the clock. "It's time for the news."

Gran and Mrs. McVeigh followed him into the living room. Trist and I put the board away.

"So who did Jasey go out with?"

Trist shook his head. "Didn't say."

"Did you ask?"

Trist sat down with an orange. "Why should I?"

I could have crammed it down his throat. "Aren't you curious?"

Trist's mouth bent in disgust. "Jasey's too full of herself. Last year she read in the library at lunch hour, or went for a run. This year, all of a sudden, she can't stand to break a sweat for fear of wrecking her makeup."

"I've got to go." I wished I'd never come. Then I wouldn't know that Jasey was out somewhere, who knew where, with people no one knew.

I must have heard every siren that night. Jasey, lying broken in a drunk's car. Jasey murdered. Jasey lost to me, forever.

FOUR

[4]

Sunday night. I heard Dad leave for work, Mom's door clicking closed. My backpack had sat unopened all weekend, a brooding green reminder of school tomorrow. I launched myself onto the bed and covered my face with the pillow.

Ms. Priestly had given me an out. I didn't have to do a written report on our novel study.

"Illustrate it."

"What?"

"Read the book. Read the images, and paint them in your own mind. Then paint them for me." She handed me a set of watercolor paints and some brushes. "Or use pencils. It's up to you."

Trist thought I'd won the lottery. "Illustrate it! You could do that in your sleep." I wasn't so sure. I'd never drawn something out of someone else's head.

I rolled the pillow off my face. The backpack had taken on a life force. It would creep toward me in the night and suffocate me in my sleep. I'd die with the smell of pencils and old apples in my nostrils. I pushed myself off the bed and hefted the pack onto my table. I opened the zipper with the same sense of dread I always have. This was going to be work.

Perils of the wild. The kid in the book faced death about seven times just in the first chapter. I thought about drawing death, a black-fanged dragon with blood in his eyes. Not quite what Ms. Priestly had in mind. I flipped to the opening chapter. The words shifted in menacing patterns on the page. I took a deep breath and read.

It's not that I can't read. Charlie Able used to crack us up the way he'd read words, switching the letters around in his head. I see the words fine. Mrs. Montgomery told me once that reading is a wonderful escape from life's troubles. Maybe, if the book has a plane ticket in it.

I tried to capture the forest and lake of the story. I imagined the road to Fort McMurray in northern Alberta where Mom's folks live. We went there once. Flew to Edmonton, then all day in their car, and nothing to see but trees. Not a fence post in sight. Just a road poked into the forest. Ten paces either way off the highway and you could be lost. It would be that simple. It was unnerving in a car. I could imagine what the boy in the story felt like.

Imagine. I drew the boy the way I imagined him, with blue eyes like Trist, and sandy brown hair. No one who gets lost in the forest has red hair like mine.

The blue eyes were wide, afraid. I smudged his face a bit for dirt, and set the mouth with a look that might say, "I am so dead."

For the forest and lake I tried the watercolors. I'd used these before in art class. They make quick work of background color. I painted the sky a thin gray, a hopeless color, like the boy. He didn't stand a chance. They were never going to find him, not before he starved or got eaten by something.

I let the paint dry on the paper, then added pencil lines to define the trees. The trees would kill him. They'd hide him from the rescue plane like a carpet hides a flea.

I yawned. It was late, past midnight. I had math homework too, but maybe I'd have time before school to do it.

I didn't have time, of course. I woke up late, then helped Mom clear up the breakfast dishes and make lunches.

"Those bologna better be for me." Blake was hunched over a bowl of cereal, his eyes following my every move.

There was bologna for two sandwiches, peanut butter for the others. I was going to put one bologna in each bag. Share them.

"Now Blake." Mom's hands went to the collar of her robe. They were pale hands, deeply lined even though my mother isn't that old. They fluttered.

Blake's eyes flashed. His lips tightened into a scowl.

"It's okay, Mom. I don't even like bologna." I put the two bologna sandwiches into Blake's bag.

"You put mustard on them?" Blake's nostrils flared, but his color was coming back to normal.

"Yes, I put mustard on them."

He pushed off his chair and grabbed the bag.

"You'll be home after school?" She'd rather have the misery of him being here than not knowing where he was.

The sound of a rumbling car exhaust announced his friend Clay's arrival. A look crossed Blake's face, just a shadow, something almost like fear. Clay inspires that in his friends. Without answering, he left, the screen door smashing against the house.

The year of Mom's accident we ate meat every night, an entire side of a pig. Bacon, chops, ham, pork in our sandwiches at lunch. It turned Mom off meat of all kinds. I was eight. I loved it.

The pig man and his wife brought the meat, frozen

lumps wrapped in brown paper. And they brought a lamp, a pig's-foot lamp, four little trotters mounted on a round wooden base.

"Is that the pig?" my mother asked, aghast. She'd hit one of their pigs on the highway the day before. Totaled the car. Totaled the pig.

Dad laughed. "Karen, how could that be the pig you killed just yesterday?" Ha ha ha, silly woman. He took the meat and loaded it into the freezer.

"It's just a little hobby of mine," said the pig man. "I like to make lamps."

"He's real handy," said the pig man's wife. "Made me a pigskin sewing basket. The handle for the lid is a piglet's tail."

Mom blanched.

My dad jerked his head at me. "Offer our guests some tea, Gavin. And see if you can do it without breaking anything." Ha ha ha.

Mom was on the couch. Her ankle was in a cast. Her voice was thin. "And find some biscuits or something in the cupboard. I'm afraid I didn't bake anything."

The pig man put the lamp on the table by the couch and plugged it in. The heat from the light bulb raised a smell off those pig feet that made me want to gag. I set down the tea and fled.

Mom's ankle took awhile to heal. She got a new Toyota, blue, with a CD player. But it just sits in the garage. Mom never goes out. The pig wasn't killed in the crash. Mom said it laid on the pavement crying like a hundred babies. A police officer had to kill it with his gun. Everyone said she was lucky *she* wasn't killed— one whole side of the car was caved in. She didn't even know she was pregnant, but when she miscarried the next month, the doctor said it probably wasn't because of the accident. Dad said it was just as well, that two kids were more than enough. It's like the accident tipped life on its side for her. Then Blake hit his teens like a fist through wallboard, and whatever energy Mom has, it goes to keeping a lid on him. The pig's-foot lamp sits on the table right where the pig man put it, although we know better than to turn it on.

If I could have seen how she was going to change, how she was going to disappear from me, I'd never have eaten that pig.

She says she still dreams about crying babies.

Mom rested her hand on my shoulder as I was loading my lunch into my pack. "You're a good boy, Gavin."

I cracked a smile for her. Gray was showing in the hair at her temples.

"Yeah, Mom." I turned to say good-bye, but she was already sitting down to the paper, her eyes intent on headlines of mayhem and disaster.

FIVE

[5]

"Basketball today." Trist shoved the last of his sandwich into his mouth, chewing around the words.

Charlie Able whined. "We were supposed to play soccer. It's my turn in goal."

"Change of plans." The others at the table didn't say anything, either because they didn't care, or because they knew it was pointless to argue with Trist. I wasn't fond of soccer or basketball, although my stunning lack of speed was less obvious when we played basketball.

"You want my milk? I'm done." He pushed the carton in front of me. I drained it quickly, trying to ignore his backwash. I was wiping my mouth on my sleeve when Alexis Denner shoved in across the table from us.

"Who wants to arm wrestle?"

A chorus of groans lifted from the table.

Alexis is probably the smartest student in eighth

grade, a fact she's happy to remind you of. She may also be the biggest.

"You're not afraid, are you?" Alexis's eyes fixed on Trist, her heavy black brows arched in confrontation.

"Only afraid of catching something."

Alexis seemed oblivious to the laughter. "Well, if you're not man enough, maybe your little friend wants to go." Her hooded eyes met mine in challenge.

I could feel the blood welling up under the roots of my hair, but I didn't care. I hate being called little. "Yeah, okay, I'll wrestle." I set my elbow on the table.

"You don't have to." Trist was smiling, but I could see the concern on his face. Alexis was likely to drive my wrist right through the table.

"No, I'll fight her. In fact, I'd like to fight her."

Marc joined the small crowd behind Alexis. "You're nuts. But you're brave to try."

"I'm with Gavin. He's bulked up some over the summer." That was Roger. He stood with Trist behind me.

I was way too far into this now. Other tables were standing up to better see the action. Alexis's friends were hooting out a cheer for her. I wanted to die, except for the puddle I'd surely leave behind. I wiped my hand on my jeans.

Alexis's face shone in anticipated victory. She set her elbow on the table, her eyebrows lifted in evil invitation. "Ready, squirt?"

"Ignore her. Keep your mind clear." Trist was rubbing my shoulders. "Just know that you can do it, and you will."

Maybe Trist could do it. It would have been nice of him to try. My hand looked pale and small next to hers. I clasped it. It was bone dry.

I closed my eyes, waiting for the signal, shutting out the jeers and chants from around the table. Trist called it.

"GO!"

I squeezed my hand, willing power into it. I felt the muscles in my arms tighten against Alexis'. My eyes clenched closed, I drove my arm against her. She was a locomotive. A polar bear. A brick wall. She was impossibly strong.

I knew how red I must be. I could feel the blood pounding at my temples. I opened my eyes a crack and risked a quick look at Alexis.

When I opened my eyes they were level with her T-shirt. I never would have looked there normally. But I opened my eyes, and there was her T-shirt, and there were two lumps under her shirt. I gasped.

I couldn't pull my eyes away. Alexis Denner had boobs!

She must have seen me looking, because I could feel the rage in her hand. Instead of pushing my hand toward the table, she started to squeeze. Her hand engulfed mine, crunching it like the jaws of a beast. The pain was incredible. My eyes filled. Still, I couldn't look away. I became aware of a low guttural moan, and was appalled that it was me. I would not cry. It would finish me for all time to let Alexis make me cry. Right then I hated Trist.

With strength born of desperation I pushed on Alexis's hand. She squeezed harder. It was like my hand wasn't there anymore, just a burning hot crumple of nerve and flesh. My stomach rolled. Sweat was running down my wrist and back and neck.

The bell rang to go outside. I felt Trist's words rather than heard them. "It's a draw!" He slapped the table. "Break. It's a draw." I let her slam my hand down.

Both sides were cheering, claiming victory. Trist clapped my shoulder and other hands thumped my back. I swiped at my face, not wanting to look at Alexis.

"She should have won." I held my hand under my arm as Trist led me out into the schoolyard. "She had me beat."

"But she didn't." Trist lobbed a basketball to Charlie. "You held her for three minutes. She would have, eventually. But you held her." He jogged under the hoop to rebound Charlie's shot.

"Great job, Gavin." More guys thumped me on the back. "I don't know how you did it."

I did. She let me.

"You not playing?" Trist called to me.

I waved my good hand at him. "No, I've got to finish my math homework."

Voices filled in behind me on the basketball court, the arm wrestle forgotten, as I pushed through the school door. The washroom was deserted, and I ran cold water over my hand until I couldn't feel it anymore.

SIX

[6]

"I found some good stuff today." Grandpa Jack shifted his popcorn and crossed his foot over his knee. "Amazing what some people will throw away."

Trist covered his mouth with his hand and sunk lower into the theater seat. We were waiting for the movie to start. James Bond. It was just the three of us. Trist said Jasey was under house arrest for breaking curfew.

"A perfectly good pair of running shoes. And just a half-size bigger than my own. I wear two pairs of socks and they fit like they were made for me."

Grandpa Jack has a route of trash cans and dump bins that he checks each day for bottles and cans.

"I had to clean them up a bit. But look, they're as good as new."

The shoes did look fine, if you could get over where he'd got them.

"Maybe you could find some for Gavin. He's

about through his." Trist was smiling, and I knew he didn't mean anything by it.

Grandpa Jack retied the shoelace, his foot dancing lightly on his knee. He looked so pleased you couldn't help but feel good for him.

"Who's to say James Bond isn't a real person?" Trist handed me a red licorice and leaned back in the seat.

"He couldn't be a real person." Grandpa Jack shoveled a handful of popcorn into his mouth. There was popcorn on his shirt, in his lap, on the floor. "If he was a real person, then they wouldn't let a movie be made about him."

"Or they would, just to make people think that he wasn't actually real."

Grandpa Jack scrabbled for another handful of popcorn. "Maybe they just want us to think he's real."

"So you're saying he's real?"

He reached across me to slap Trist playfully on the side of the head, laughing a great, booming laugh.

The trailers came on and Grandpa Jack leaned forward in his seat. I'd have hated to be the person sitting behind him, the way he fidgeted. We watched the movie, hooting and laughing, and I didn't mind that Jasey didn't come, because we could be guys.

In the car on the way home, Trist and Grandpa Jack debated who was the best James Bond of all time. Grandpa Jack drives an old Caddie, not the kind of car you'd expect a guy who goes through Dumpsters to drive. Gran says it's ostentatious.

"That means showy," Trist had explained.

I know what it means. I don't have a Webster's definition. It's the kind of spelling word that would give me bad dreams. But I KNOW what it means. I wear Blake's old jackets and sneakers that my toes push through, but I have the best bike in the rack. It's important to Grandpa Jack to have a proper vehicle. I know what that means.

"Hey, you guys have to hear my new disc player!" Grandpa Jack slid a CD into a player under the dash. "Gran nearly had heart failure when I told her what I paid." A guitar twanged from the speakers and some forlorn cowboy wailed to the moon. "Probably two years of collecting bottles and cans, and worth every penny."

It did sound good, even the cowboy music. Trist nodded his head in time to the music and Grandpa Jack hummed as he drove.

When I got home, Dad was in his chair, a beer in his hand and an empty beside him. Tuesday was his night off, and he'd be going to the bar. His eyes were shiny.

"How did you pay for that movie?"

The beers he'd drunk were just to warm up. He

would come home reeking so badly of booze that the house would stink for days.

"It was only a couple of bucks. I had it from walking Mr. Bowen's dogs."

Dad leaned forward, his eyes an ugly squint.

"You didn't maybe find that money somewhere? Like, on my dresser?"

A ring of sweat prickled my neck like a steel collar. "What are you talking about?"

He snorted, swigging from his beer as he eyed me over the rim of the can. "Someone emptied my change jar. Lightened my load by about twenty bucks."

I swallowed. "Well, it wasn't me."

Dad swung toward me in his chair. His face had turned gray, and his mouth twisted in a sneer. "Well, it wasn't me." He used a high falsetto voice to imitate mine.

Blood was pounding into my cheeks. "What makes you think I stole it?"

"Don't talk to me like that, boy."

I knew it was dangerous, but I didn't care. Why would he think I'd taken his money when we shared a house with Blake the Bandit? "No. Tell me."

Dad lurched out of his chair. A bright white light shot through my eyes as the back of his hand crashed into my cheek. I dropped to the floor and covered my head.

I heard Mom's slippers making a fast path to the living room just as the back door opened. From under my elbow I could see Dad's big feet, and behind him, Mom, clutching her robe. Then Blake walked into the room.

Dad's feet turned away from me to Blake, and I lifted my head. I blinked twice to clear my vision, then blinked again. Blake had tossed himself into Dad's chair and was clicking through the channels with the TV remote.

I almost laughed. No one sat in Dad's chair, not when he was home, and not if there was a chance of him getting home soon. Blake pulled the lever on the side of the chair, and the footrest swung up under his sneakers.

Something like a snort came out of Dad's mouth, but he didn't make a move. Mom was all eyes, her jaw hanging loose.

They were new, Blake's sneakers, and nice ones too. He pulled a cell phone out of his shirt pocket and set it on the table by the chair.

That made me want to laugh too. Clay must have given him the phone, and probably the shoes. Nice work if you can get it. Something told me they weren't delivering pizza.

Blake drummed his fingers on the table, and I half expected him to take a swig of Dad's beer. But then he swung his gaze from the TV, looked around as if he hadn't noticed us before, and said, "What?"

His eyes were red-rimmed and glassy. Maybe he really hadn't seen us.

I glanced up at Dad. He was standing there, perfectly baffled, like a bear that finds itself suddenly in the glare of headlights.

"You're in my chair." He took a step toward Blake but then stepped back.

Blake looked down at the arms of the chair, processing that bit of information. "You're right." He turned back to the TV and changed channels.

Suicidal. He had to be.

"Well, I want it back!" Dad's hands clenched at his sides.

Blake found the music channel and notched up the volume.

Definite death wish.

Dad took two steps toward Blake and bellowed, "Get out of my freakin' chair!"

Blake clicked off the TV and calmly stepped out of the chair, leaving the footrest up. "Oh, were you using it?" His face expressionless, Blake handed Dad the remote and sauntered into the kitchen.

"Sitting there like a dog." Dad wasn't looking at me, but I knew all the same that he was talking to me. He dropped into the chair with a grunt. "Get me a beer."

Blake was at the fridge, draining a beer. I reached in beside him and got another one out.

"Thanks for distracting him. He would have beat the crap out of me."

He finished the beer, crumpled the can, and belched. His eyes fixed on me and narrowed. "You're a stupid puke. Like I'd do anything to help you." He flicked his wrist and the beer can struck me in the face. With that he turned and left the house.

SEVEN

[7]

Ever since the arm wrestle I couldn't look at Alexis, and maybe that was good, because she left me alone too. I could hardly hold a pen for an entire week after she crushed my hand, and even now when I think of her it aches.

Ms. Priestly liked the artwork I did for the novel study, and I've done three more chapters. It's weird—when I'm drawing that boy, it's like I can feel his fear, his loneliness. And I've been dreaming about bears.

I pushed open the back door and slung my pack up onto a hook. The kitchen was dark, which was strange because that's where my mother spends her day. Voices rumbled from Blake's room in the basement. He was home. My stomach sunk and rolled in one green motion.

From the sounds, there were more than a few guys down there. I heard laughter, then one voice lifted above the others. Clay's.

"There's always more. More of everything." Then, "Just make sure you collect, and don't jerk me around."

The bathroom door off the kitchen opened and a tall skinny guy with bleary eyes emerged, tucking in his shirt. His gaze fell on me and something like despair flitted across his face. He thudded down the stairs and immediately the voices stopped.

I heard footsteps coming back up, and Blake's dark face met mine. "What do you think you're doing?"

I gulped and stuttered, "N-Nothing."

He shoved me against the door. His eyes were flat and glassy. "How long have you been standing there? What did you hear?"

Clay slid in behind him, the others moving out of his way. "Relax." He set his hand on Blake's shoulder. "We were just leaving anyway."

He was a year or two older than Blake, blond, really bad skin. His shirt was open at the collar and a gold chain gleamed on his chest. Blake shut up instantly.

"We'll discuss this later." Clay motioned for the others to follow him. He held the door as they filed out, their eyes, like Blake's, shiny and stupid. He looked at me for a minute, his eyes mere slits, his mouth curling into a smile. My guts gurgled and turned. He lifted his finger, pointing it at me like a gun. "Be seeing you." Then he looked back at Blake and the smile disappeared. He let the door close with a quiet click.

Blake shoved past me to the fridge.

"Where's Mom?" I hated the squeal in my voice.

Blake looked at me with eyes that didn't want to focus. He reminded me of Dad when he drank. "The old lady?" A shadow of a smile crossed his face. Then he frowned. "She had to go out."

"Out?" That was an image, Mom in her robe and slippers leaving the house.

"It's sad, really." He covered his face with both hands. "Poor little Tiger."

I grabbed the counter. "What about Tiger?" I tried to keep my voice calm. Tiger is really my cat. He sleeps on my pillow. Sometimes when I'm drawing, he sits on my paper. He likes the way the pencil moves.

"A dog got him. His insides were on the outside."

I felt like someone had kicked me. I forced my mouth to work. "Where is he?"

"Mom took him to the vet. To be put down."

I turned so he wouldn't see me cry. My legs barely made the stairs, and I collapsed on my bed. There was a soft round recess in the pillow where Tiger had last slept. I put my face into the pillow like I could breathe him back into me.

I sobbed silently, so that no one would hear me. I sobbed until my ribs wanted to break. She should have waited. I would have taken him. Then I could have said good-bye. He was my cat. I wailed silently into the pillow.

The room was dark when I woke up. The pillow was wet from where I'd been crying and my eyes felt sore and puffed. I lay there, every shred of strength gone from me.

"Your supper's getting cold." Mom's voice came through the door like nails.

How could she even think about eating? "I'm not coming."

"You'll do what your mother tells you to." Dad's voice came from his bedroom. I got up.

The light in the kitchen stung my eyes, and I slid onto my chair hardly seeing it. Blake was at the table, a rare occurrence. His head was down, his hands in his lap. Mom was at the stove, in her robe, stabbing sausages onto plates.

"Gavin, one sausage or two?"

I waved them off. "I can't eat."

Mom set down the plate and put her hand on my forehead. "What, are you sick?"

Take a cat and its entrails to the vet, have it put down, then serve sausages and mashed potatoes for dinner. I pushed her hand away. "No, I'm not sick."

"Well, then, what is it?" She went to the fridge and set the milk on the counter. Then she reached in, took out an open can of cat food, sniffed it, and tossed it in the trash.

A gasp escaped me. I glanced at Blake. He was bolting his food, jamming the sausages down practically whole.

Mom came back to the table with the milk. I said to her, "You don't think I might be a little upset?"

She lifted her shoulders. "What?"

Blake pushed back from the table. He looked strange, his mouth twisted. At first I thought he was scowling. Then I saw. He was trying not to smile. Hairs lifted on my arms one by one.

"Where are you going?" Mom said to his back.

"Out." He slammed the door.

I turned to Mom, gripping her bony arm with my hand. "Where were you when I got home after school?"

She pulled away and tugged on the belt of her robe. "Oh, honey, I told Blake to tell you. I was napping."

"So you didn't go out today? Anywhere?" My voice shook and I was going to cry, but I couldn't help it.

"No, of course not. Gavin, what's wrong with you?"

"Where's Tiger?" A huge sob caught in my throat, and I hiccuped. Acid tears filled my eyes.

"Well I don't know. He was on the back of the couch the last time I saw him."

"What's his problem?" Dad came into the kitchen, doing up his pants.

I pushed past him to the living room. Tiger raised one sleepy eye to look at me when I lifted him off the couch. "Oh, Tiger." He strained away from my wet face. I drank in his dusty smell.

Outside, in the front yard, Blake was leaning on the lamppost, laughing. He was watching me, laughing so hard that he put his hands on his knees. A blue sports car pulled up, Clay's car, and he got in, still laughing as it tore away from the curb.

EIGHT

[8]

Gran collects family pictures, and they rest like fall leaves on the mantle, piano, shelves, TV, any available surface. She even has my school picture in a frame. It was never a conscious decision, theirs or mine, I don't think, to adopt me into this family. Gran used to babysit me before I started school. Then Trist moved in. Now, after years of my spending most afternoons here, every weekend, and all summer, the McVeighs just take me on as one of their own. I'm not in their family picture, but I carry their house key on the same chain as my own. And this living room, with its fuzzy brown furniture and old wood, and the magazine table by the couch filled with *Field and Stream* and crossword books, is so imprinted on my mind that when I'm at home and get up in the night, I stumble around until I realize where I am.

Trist's father's picture has a place of honor on the mantle beside Gran's antique candlesticks. He was good looking, his blue eyes like Trist's and Jasey's, his smile reaching out from the frame.

"That's a face only a mother could love." Grandpa Jack looked over my shoulder at the photo. It was his face all over again, the long strong nose, the chiseled lips. The eyes were the same too, although right then Grandpa Jack's looked sad.

"You must miss him."

He smiled, and patted me on the shoulder. "Yes, I miss him."

"Do you think Trist's mom will ever remarry?"

He took his time answering. "It's hard for her to meet people, living with us, the parents of her dead husband. Not that we'd stop her. She's always been like a daughter." He raked his fingers through his silver hair. "And she works hard. Long hours. Saving for college tuition, you know."

I looked at him, surprised. "Dad says she's loaded."

Grandpa Jack lifted his chin. "Does he now."

I could feel myself blushing, the bluntness of my comment hanging like a bad smell. "I just meant the insurance money. From the accident." Trist's father had worked on a fishing trawler. Something happened and he went overboard.

Grandpa Jack crossed his arms over his chest. "There's not always insurance money."

He took the picture of Sam McVeigh down off the mantle, wiping a bit of dust from the top of it. His eyes traced the photo, almost like he was searching for something just out of view.

"His body was never found."

I watched his face, wondering what you say to a man who has outlived his son.

"We had a funeral for him, but the casket was empty. There was nothing to bury. So we just buried our heartache." He sighed, his shoulders drooping with the weight of his thoughts.

"I'm really sorry."

He didn't look at me. It was like he'd forgotten I was there. He stood staring at the picture, chewing his lips. Then his eyes hardened. It made me uncomfortable to look at him.

"He had everything. A good job. A wife who loved him. Two great kids. Life was good to him." He set the picture frame down with an angry thump. The harshness of the movement made me jump.

"Two lines scribbled on a scrap of paper. 'I'm sorry. I wish I could be stronger.' Two measly lines to sum up his life. Then he ends it."

My mouth was suddenly dry, and my words came out as a whisper. "I didn't know."

He looked at me then, and it was like he was puzzled for a moment, like he didn't know who I was.

"Then I guess I shouldn't have told you. It's not something we talk about, not normally." He straightened his shoulders. "But anyway, there was no insurance."

I felt like a fool for blurting out about the money. I tried to recover. "But Trist's smart. He could get into any school just on his brains. Jasey too."

"They're smart enough. And you're no dummy yourself."

"Dad says …" I stopped myself before I finished. Dad says it'll be a miracle if I get through high school.

"Well, we've already determined that your dad doesn't know everything," Grandpa Jack said, reading my mind.

I couldn't tell Grandpa Jack that what I wanted was to go to art school, that I wanted to paint book covers and pictures that people would hang in their homes. I couldn't tell him that, because Dad was more right than he was. I was terrible at school.

He set his hand again on his son's picture. "I'm not saying your dad doesn't know a thing or two. I'm sure he does. But he only knows what he knows. You can draw from that what you need. And you can throw away the rest." His hands trembled slightly on the picture frame. "Be careful you don't throw away the good stuff, Gavin. No matter how bad it seems, you've always got a choice."

NINE
[9]

Grandpa Jack had built Trist a tree fort in the backyard, and while we were far too mature to play Vikings anymore, with fake swords and blood and guts, we still liked to sit up there and ponder life. It had a straight-on view to the upstairs bathroom window, and Jasey had just gone in.

"It's almost noon. She's been sleeping all this time?" It was a stupid question. Blake has been known to spend entire days in bed.

"She's grounded again. Didn't get home until almost 2:00. Mom was phoning all the hospitals ..."

"2:00 in the morning! What the heck did she say she was she doing?"

Trist looked at me and rolled his eyes. "Oh, she'd be telling them that. Over bacon and waffles. 'Well, folks, first I drank my face off, then smoked some drugs, then I got into a guy's car ...'"

"Shut up!" My voice lifted over the tree fort. The

bathroom window slammed closed.

Trist's voice shook. "What do you think she was doing? Studying at the library? You are so naïve."

Maybe I am. But what was happening to Jasey? She used to like being at home, watching movies, playing Monopoly. She used to like being with us. She even liked being with Uncle Pat, and that wasn't easy to do.

When he'd moved to the home, it was Jasey who'd insisted we visit him. "If you were trapped in a wheelchair, you'd want someone to come and see you."

The home is for people with his disease. Huntington's disease. There are people of all ages in the home. We'd find Uncle Pat in a sitting area on the patio, his chair turned to catch the light. Gran would bustle around, chatting with the staff, chirping greetings to the other residents.

One time a woman in a chair sucked a cigarette held to her lips by a young woman sitting beside her. Her head lurched as she took the smoke into her lungs, the cigarette glowing bright red as she pulled on it. She let the smoke out in a cloud, something like a smile on her face. The young woman giggled.

"They're sisters." Gran spoke quietly to me. I must have been staring. I yanked my eyes away. "They probably smoked together behind the garage, too."

In another life.

Gran spooned vanilla ice cream into Uncle Pat's gaping mouth. It trickled down one side of his chin.

"I'd shoot myself before they put me in a place like this," Trist muttered. I followed his gaze to a man about my father's age, bent into a chair. He was thin, like many of the people in the chairs, his hair combed over papery skin. He didn't lurch like the others, but his hands curled the same way, and his head swayed as he watched us.

"He probably has kids our age," Jasey said. She smiled at the man.

The man's mouth stretched wide, then clamped closed.

"He's smiling! Look!"

"How do you know it's not just gas?" Trist sniffed the air suspiciously.

"I'm going over there." Jasey smoothed the front of her shirt and shifted the curls on her shoulders. Trist and I watched open-mouthed as she made her way to the man in the chair.

"Hello. I'm Jasey McVeigh." She extended her hand. The man in the chair blinked. A large woman in a pink smock appeared at his side, someone on staff.

"This is Mr. Dinning." The woman took the man's hand and folded it over Jasey's. "Mr. Dinning designs planes."

In another life. The woman in the smock turned to another resident. Jasey pulled a chair next to the man, his hand still around hers.

"I've been to the Boeing plant," she said, and she sat with him, chatting. She was there for an hour, and Trist and I were ready to die of boredom, but she seemed genuinely happy to be with him.

I shifted on the floor of the tree fort and leaned toward Trist. "Has Jasey talked to you?"

"Jasey's changed, Gavin. I don't even know her anymore."

My stomach dropped. "You think she's in trouble?"

Trist looked at me, hard, and he kept looking at me. It made me uncomfortable, but I held his stare. He said, "She's got different friends."

"That doesn't mean anything." I knew I sounded desperate.

"She doesn't go running in the morning. She goes over to her friend's house to change into the clothes she really wants to wear to school. The clothes Mom or Gran would never allow her to buy. The clothes that make her look like a slut."

"Maybe she's got a job. Maybe that's why she's out late." My voice was small.

"Get over it, Gavin. She may as well be someone else."

"How did this happen? I mean, she was fine all

53

summer, wasn't she? How could she change so fast?"

Trist crossed his arms and shook his head. He stared at the bathroom window, his jawbone flexing like he was chewing on his thoughts. Then he turned to me, slowly, and said, "Maybe you don't really want to know."

TEN
[10]

Dad came home from work with a huge dog, one of Mr. Murphy's guard dogs, a broad-shouldered thick-jawed thing with streaks of dark brown in its mud-colored coat. A pit bull. We were all in the kitchen and must have been standing with our mouths open because he blurted, "It's a dog. D.O.G. Dog." He brought it in and unclipped its leash. Blake backed up toward the door; Tiger disappeared under the couch; I pressed myself against the wall.

"Oh. A dog." Mom's voice was tentative, but she extended her hand for the dog to sniff. A low growl rumbled in its throat. She pulled her hand back and set it at her collar. "What's its name?"

"Bunny."

"Bunny!" Blake snorted through his nose. The dog tilted its massive head in his direction. Blake stopped laughing.

"She whined when I went to put her in the kennel.

Old man Murphy told me to take her home. Figures he can tell me to do anything and I'll do it." He reached his hand down and the dog pushed its nose into it. "Now I'm his dog rehab program." Dad looked at me. "Come say hello to her. So she'll know you."

I swallowed.

"You don't have anything to be afraid of. She won't go for you unless I tell her to."

The dog was sniffing the air in my direction. Tasting it.

"Come here." Dad's voice was firm. I went.

"Let her smell your hand."

I could hear Blake snickering behind me. I held my hand out to the dog. Its dull brown eyes stayed on mine as it sniffed me. Its hot exhaled breath hit my palm in a cloud. Then it stuck its nose right into my hand, and its stubby tail thumped on the floor.

I breathed.

"See? She likes you." Dad clapped me on the back.

"Let me try again." Mom stretched out her hand to the dog. It sniffed it and growled.

Dad laughed. "I guess you smell like the criminal type. Now your turn, Blake."

Blake jammed his hands in his pockets. "I don't want to."

The smile disappeared from Dad's face. "I didn't ask you if you wanted to. Get over here."

"No." He sounded less sure.

Dad sucked in a breath and let it out slowly. "You're a chicken. Bunny likes chicken. Likes it raw on the bone." A smile twitched at the corners of his mouth. "You better let her have a sniff of you, or she's not going to know you belong here. She's likely to think you're an intruder. And you wouldn't want that."

The color drained from Blake's face and sweat beaded his forehead. He pulled his hands from his pockets, wiping his palms. Slowly he approached the dog. I could see his hand shaking as he reached out.

Dad grinned, then with perverse calmness commanded, "Sic 'im!"

The dog lunged at Blake's arm, closing its immense jaw around his wrist, a noise like the devil emerging from its throat.

Blake gaped, his eyes wide, his breath going in but not out. Mom shrieked.

"Off!" Dad commanded.

The dog released Blake. I turned away, not wanting to see the meat of his arm. Dad was laughing.

"See? She can't hurt you."

I looked at Blake's arm. It was slimy from the dog's mouth, but unmarked.

Mom let out a sigh of relief. Blake laughed, a fake laugh, like he'd never been scared at all.

"She's got bad teeth," Dad explained. "Hurts her

to close down on things. The last guy fed her cara-
mels. Rotted her jaw." He laughed a silly tee hee.
"You should have seen your face."

"Yeah," Blake said. "I'm sure that made your day."

It made mine.

Still laughing, Dad headed for the bedroom,
Bunny at his side.

"Oh no, you're not coming in here, stinking up
my room. Lay down there and go to sleep." He pointed
to the floor outside his door. The dog obeyed. He
made a chicken clucking noise at Blake, then closed
his bedroom door behind him.

We loaded three bags of leaves into the trunk of the
Caddie, the late afternoon sun thin on our sweaty necks.

"You boys ready for a milkshake?" Grandpa Jack
rolled down his sleeves, brushing bits of leaf from the
front of his shirt. "We'll drop the leaves at the compost depot, then go to Peter's. My treat."

"Yes!" Trist held up his hand for a high-five. Peter's makes the best milkshakes in the city, so thick it
hurts your cheeks to suck them up the straw.

"Go wash up."

Jasey was at the table when we went into the
house. Her eyes were sunk in dark sockets, and she
was pale.

Trist headed into the bathroom. At the kitchen sink, I took a big yellow bar out of the soap dish and scoured my hands. Then I pushed up my sleeves and scrubbed my arms.

"You about to do surgery or something?"

I glanced at her. She was wearing a T-shirt over her jeans, her hair gathered into a loose knot. Her bare feet were tucked up on the chair. She was watching me with those haunted eyes. I thought her hands were shaking a bit.

"Cardiology," I said, then blushed bright red.

"As in broken hearts?" She smiled faintly. "Sorry, doc, I wish it were that simple. I'm afraid the patient is incurable and untreatable." She set her head in her hands, and the knot of hair slipped over one shoulder. "This patient's days are numbered."

I stood there, drying my hands on the dishtowel, watching her. I wondered what it would feel like to take her in my arms, right here in the kitchen, what her neck would smell like, the softness of her skin, the feel of her hair as I pulled it out of its knot.

"Wake up, dreamer." A wet washcloth hit me in the face. Trist laughed. I held the cloth over my face until the red subsided. "I'd like to get that milkshake before my voice changes."

Jasey raised her head. "Grandpa Jack taking you to Peter's?"

"Maybe."

"Yes," I said, my voice so eager I blushed again. "You want to come?"

"She didn't rake leaves."

"Grandpa Jack wouldn't mind."

"And she's grounded. As usual."

"I can't go anyway." Jasey lifted herself off the chair. "I've got a few phone calls to make."

"Oh. Right," I said. "Getting your affairs in order, and all that."

She smiled at me. "But thanks anyway." She tousled my hair as she passed me. "Red is a good color on you."

My cheeks flooded. It was a curse, this blushing.

Grandpa Jack was waiting for us in the car, his window rolled down, arm resting on the ledge. He had his cowboy music playing and was tapping time on the steering wheel. Trist screwed up his face and climbed in the front seat.

"You have a problem with this music?"

"No. Except when I score low on the SATs, I can blame it on the cell loss suffered listening to old country and western CDs."

"Maybe milkshakes are bad for brain cells." Grandpa Jack pulled away from the curb.

"No way. Milkshakes actually increase your capacity to learn. The Aztecs invented them, you know."

I sank into the plush back seat of the Caddie, letting their banter wash over me.

"Holy lightning!" Grandpa Jack hooted. "It's a new Dumpster!" The car screeched to a halt near a bright yellow garbage bin. He undid his seat belt.

"You're not going to search it, are you?" Trist was looking all around the car, afraid, no doubt, that someone he knew was nearby.

"I'll only be a jiff. I just want to see what kind of junk is in it."

"Oh, mercy," Trist wailed. "What about the milkshakes?"

Grandpa Jack jogged over to the Dumpster. Trist scrunched low in the seat.

"You ever wonder why Grandpa Jack goes through garbage?"

Trist's voice was muffled by the upholstery. "I try not to dwell on it."

"He didn't always go through garbage bins."

Trist poked his head over the back of the seat. "What are you getting at?"

"Nothing."

"Yes, you are." His mouth clamped tight in anger.

"Why are you so mad? I was just asking."

He was silent for a minute, then said, "There's nothing wrong with him. It's not like he has a disease or something."

I thought of Uncle Pat in the nursing home, how the ice cream trickles out of his mouth.

"Did I say he did? I don't think so!"

Trist watched out his window as Grandpa Jack up- ended himself into the Dumpster. His jaw clenched.

"Jasey thinks he's got it," he said.

I sat up in the back seat. "Huntington's disease?" Not Grandpa Jack. "Why?"

He snorted in disgust. "Says he's got mood swings."

I thought of Blake, and my father, and my mother, and me. "Everyone has mood swings."

"And she says he's starting to get the same kind of movements as Uncle Pat. And that he's forgetting things."

I swallowed hard. "You don't think he's got it, do you?"

He laughed, but his face was still angry. "Of course he doesn't have it. She doesn't know what she's talking about."

I sat back. "So, do you think that's why she's been acting so weird?"

"Why would that make her act weird?"

"Well, because if she thinks Grandpa Jack has it, then your dad could have had it."

"He's dead. He's not worrying about it."

"Yeah, but then you guys could get it too."

His jaw tightened. "Who cares why Jasey is so weird? All I know is she's wrong. Dead wrong. And I'm glad you think she's wrong too." The threat in his voice was unmistakable. "Because Grandpa Jack doesn't have it. And I'm not going to get it. That's what's true."

Grandpa Jack lumbered back to the car with a lidded crate of some kind on his shoulder. He opened the trunk and set it in, then slid in behind the wheel.

"What did you find, a coffin?" Trist asked him, his voice cheerful if a little forced.

"It's a perfectly good wooden box. Solid, feels like hardwood, too."

"What do you suppose was in it?" Trist assumed a ghoulish expression. "Body parts?"

"Somebody probably stored their LPs in it. Now, we should think about getting our milkshakes."

"And some fries."

"Maybe."

"What the heck are LPs?"

ELEVEN

[11]

The boy in the book wasn't looking so good. He was living on fish and berries, and he was getting thin. I sketched deep hollows under his cheekbones. I thought about drawing the hundreds of mosquito bites he had on his face and neck, but they would look too much like zits. I made him good and dirty.

The aspen were starting to turn, and I tinged the leaves with a little gold. It would be cold where he was. I thinned the sky, washing the sun into dilute streaks.

The kid was actually hopeful. Hopeful that someone would remember him. That someone would be smart enough to figure out where he was, and care enough to try and find him. I was tempted to draw buildings in behind the trees, but I didn't. That would have been my metaphor, not the author's.

"It's a metaphor." I remembered standing at my desk, talking to the class. Vanessa sat with her mouth wide open. I didn't often offer much to the discussion.

"The forest and the lake is like his life. If the forest was his neighborhood, he'd have people around him, but he'd still be alone. And he might not die of hunger, but he could still starve to death."

Ms. Priestly smiled at me like I'd given her a birthday present or something.

Vanessa gaped. "I don't get it."

I sat back down, feeling my face flood but not really caring.

Ms. Priestly displayed one of my paintings in the library case along with a copy of the book.

"The boy's hair is darker than that." Alexis poked a grubby finger at my work. "And he's taller."

"Only in your dreams." Trist patted his heart dramatically.

"Death by starvation would be too good for you." She pointed her nose at the ceiling and stalked off.

Troy and Marc were twisted that I was excused from the written work on the book. They said they were just as stupid as I was and they never got any breaks. Alexis didn't contest that.

"We're doing the cow eyeball in Science. Want to team up?" It was Roger. He was one of the class "producers," brilliant like Trist, but a little uptight. I glanced at Trist and he shrugged.

"Sure. We need one more to make a foursome."

Ms. Priestly taught this class too. We scanned the room, looking for a fourth perfect partner for the eyeball project. Someone with a steady hand. A strong stomach. Brains would be a nice bonus.

"I'd like each group to have at least one boy and one girl in it," Ms. Priestly intoned over the class-room hubbub.

We looked at one another. "Alexis."

She was clustered with Vanessa and two other girls, their faces showing panic as we approached. Trist spoke for us. "Alexis, you're in our group."

Vanessa tittered crazily, clutching her golden curls like they were about to drop out. "Now we need one more in our group."

Trist cast his eyes to a huddle of guys in the corner. "Troy. You're with them."

"Not Troy," Vanessa whined. "His writing is too messy."

"Maybe you'd rather have Charlie?"

Charlie Able picks his nose and eats it. He'd be a real adventure with a cow eyeball.

"No. Troy's good. We'll take Troy."

Alexis, abandoned by her friends, walked deject-edly to our corner of the room. "I'm not cutting it. And if you think I am ..."

"No, I'll cut it," Roger burst in. His eyes were

shiny with excitement.

"You'd like to, wouldn't you?" Trist screwed up his face in disgust.

Roger was all but licking his lips. I stood as far away as possible from Alexis, waiting for the eyeball.

Ms. Priestly gave her "responsible scientist" speech, then brought out the trays. Apparently, responsible scientists don't laugh or make gagging noises.

"They'll roll a bit on the tray," Ms. Priestly said.

Marc's hit the floor with a damp splat.

"Ooooh!" Vanessa shrieked and climbed onto her chair.

"It's not going to get you." Marc scrabbled on the floor to retrieve the eyeball. As he grabbed it, it squirted out of his grasp. Two more girls jumped on their chairs, and so did Jordie, a boy with round eyes and a designer haircut.

"Wash it off and put it on your tray." Ms. Priestly had a bit of an edge in her voice. A fat strand of yellow hair was hanging over her eyes. Marc snagged the eyeball under a desk, and tossed it in the sink.

"Look how slimy it is when it's wet," Marc giggled. Half the class rushed to the sink to see it. The other half shrieked.

"Students, if you would please return to your stations ..."

I felt for Ms. Priestly. Maybe she'd had to go to the

stockyard for these eyeballs. Maybe she'd had to bring them back in her car, on the front seat, in a big zipper bag. Maybe they'd been looking at her, all these eyes.

I leaned over ours in the tray. Roger was hovering protectively, the sharp knife held ready to slice open the eyeball. I put my finger on the eyeball and gently pushed. It yielded, the colored part pressing out. I turned it on the tray to examine it. It wasn't one shade of brown, but more like scales of color laid up on each other: black, browns, reds, even bits of blue and green. I imagined the eye when it was still in the cow, and pictured the fear in that eye as the cold end of a gun pressed against its skull. My stomach flopped and I stepped back from the tray.

Charlie Able took the knife in his group, no surprise. Roger handled his deftly, slicing one clean cut all around the eyeball. I sketched the results, and Alexis wrote down our observations. Trist followed the study sheet and figured out what we were supposed to be looking for. Vanessa turned green and had to leave the room.

After we cleared away the trays, we filled in the report. I used Alexis's colored pencils, because she has the big set with all the fancy colors. Ms. Priestly glued her hair back into place and sat with her hands on the arms of her chair, taking big breaths.

"This looks good." Trist underlined the headings

with a red pen. "We even got the challenge questions."

That was a first for me.

"And no one puked." We all looked over at Vanessa. She had her head on her desk.

"Aren't you glad you were in our group?" Trist prodded Alexis in the arm with the pen.

Her eyebrows shot up. She looked first at him, then longer at me, and with the smallest of smiles she said, "Aren't you glad you were in mine?"

TWELVE

"I need my gloves. We'll have to swing back by my house to get them." It was cold, and my knuckles felt stiff on the handlebars. Trist buckled his helmet and didn't say anything. We never went to my house.

"Blake will still be in bed. I just have to get my gloves. Come on."

He swung his leg over his bike and shrugged. "I'm not afraid of that goon."

Yeah, right. I'm sure there was a time when Blake was human. Maybe even nice. Probably when he was about a minute old. Mom has stacks of photo albums of him as a baby. Dad even has a framed picture of him on his dresser. In the picture, Blake is sitting on Dad's shoulders. But even before Blake got evil, he'd terrorize Trist and me. Once, ages ago, he hid in my closet. Must have been in there an hour, absolutely silent. Trist and I were playing Lego. I opened the closet door for something and Blake leaped out. Trist screamed like he was being killed, and that woke up my dad. Dad came charging into the room wearing just his underwear, his face all red and his hands big fists at his sides. He belted me in the side of the head, kicked Blake in the butt as he was fleeing, and would have hit Trist too, I think, if Mom hadn't rescued us. You don't wake up my father.

You probably wouldn't want to wake up Bunny, either. Bunny the pit bull sleeps in Dad's room now. She goes with him on his rounds. Mom commented about the dog hair on his uniform and Dad was almost sheepish—said he let the dog sit in the front seat sometimes.

The cold air stuck in my throat. It was getting late in the year to ride. We liked to bike a loop around the south end of the city and out to the secondary road in the country. There it felt like we were in a different world, with the rolling fields and little knots of aspen trees. I could ride that road forever.

I set my bike up against the house. Trist tossed me his water bottle.

"Fill it for me, will you?"

I tossed it back. "Do it yourself."

Trist sighed and swung off his bike. He followed me into the kitchen.

Mom was at the table with the newspaper, circling something in red pen. She closed it quickly when we came in.

"That robe's a nice color on you, Mrs. Frisk."

Mom smiled at Trist. She patted back her hair.

"I'll just grab my gloves."

Even before I got back to the kitchen I sensed there was trouble. Blake has some kind of electro-magnetic field, and the air in the house was buzzing.

"Why do you have to be that way, Blake?" My mom was clutching at her robe, her eyes wide. Trist was leaning up against the sink, a can of Pepsi in his hand, a look of sheer terror on his face. Blake was two inches away from him, wearing just a pair of jeans, the muscles in his back bunching up.

"He took the last pop. It was mine."

"I gave it to him. Now just go back downstairs."

Blake turned on her. His skin looked like flour and water, his eyes were deeply sunken and lined with red. His whole body was trembling, like he was sick.

"Don't tell me what to do." He hurled a wad of green spit on the floor at her feet. "It wasn't yours to give away."

I felt my hands ball up into fists. "Leave her alone."

He spun toward me. Trist edged his way toward the door.

"That's enough, boys. You don't want to wake up Dad."

"And since when do you own all the pop? It's not like you buy it."

Mom was looking at me like I'd lost my mind. I never took on Blake.

He crossed the kitchen in two steps, pushed his hand against my chin, and smashed me into the fridge. Magnets flew off onto the floor, followed by bits of shopping lists and business cards for furnace cleaners.

"Who asked for your opinion?" He released my head, then thumped it again into the fridge. The heel of his hand was against my throat, and I could feel my windpipe closing off. My feet left the floor. My eyes were probably bugging out.

"Let me down." It came out like a whisper.

Mom took the broom and beat it across his back. This was all in silence, of course, because we didn't, any of us, want to wake Dad. Blake grabbed the broom with his free hand and snapped it under his foot.

Trist was looking like he might cry. Big help that would be. My throat felt like spaghetti, and I was barely getting any air. Mom was fussing about the broken broom. Trist was standing there like a doorknob. And Blake was pushing harder.

I am not an athlete. I'm too short for basketball and volleyball, too slow for football and soccer, too stupid for racquet sports. But my legs are strong. I brought one knee up, hard, into the sensitive part of my brother's anatomy. He dropped me like a brick.

He crumpled to the floor, holding himself. I fell

too, my breath returning in ragged bursts. Mom fluttered. "I'll get some ice."

Trist's hand was over his mouth, to stop from either screaming or laughing, I couldn't tell which. I pushed myself off the floor and bolted for the door. "Come on." My voice sounded like a tape played backwards. "We don't want to be here when he gets up."

Trist didn't need any encouragement. He pushed through the door in front of me, leaped on his bike, and was pedaling down the street to save his life. I caught up with him.

He looked at me, his eyes still wild. "You've got blood under your nose."

I swiped it with my hand. Not much blood. It could have been worse. I grinned at him. "You want to race?"

"Is your voice going to stay like that?" He stood on his pedals and surged ahead. That was okay. I'd just let him tire a little, then I'd gear up and leave him in the dust. I didn't even want to think about going home again.

THIRTEEN

[13]

Roger has been helping me in math. He just *gets* math. He can look at a problem and know right away what equation to write for it. Trist is like that too. But Trist has never been able to teach me. I think it's because it's so automatic for Trist that he doesn't really know how he came up with the answer. Mrs. McVeigh worked with me until I was too embarrassed to ask her to help me. But she was good. She got me through the multiplication tables in third grade.

Roger came from Taiwan, and he had to learn English. I think that's why he can teach me. He knows what it's like to have to learn something everyone else knows.

"You're not that stupid," he said, surprise in his voice. "You figured out these questions and only got a few wrong."

"Yeah, but you helped me."

"Not that much. Maybe you have to memorize

what I know, but so what? At least you're getting the right answers."

He marked the score on the top of the page: 17 out of 20. I tried not to look too pleased.

"I could come to your house to help you again, after school sometime."

"No, you can't."

He looked hurt. He doesn't have many friends.

"I mean, my dad works nights, and he needs quiet so he can sleep."

He shrugged. "Then come to my place. You can be as noisy as you like doing math."

Mrs. Stang, the math teacher, looked over our shoulders at the math sheet. "Good work. Gavin, you can get a practice sheet from the shelf under the window and take it home."

The window in Mrs. Stang's classroom looks out on the field between our school and the high school. The field was deserted now, just wrappers blowing around. The sky was gray and fell to the schoolyard like a damp blanket. It was flat and dense, with not even the black of storm clouds to make you think there was anything behind the gray.

I glanced over to the high school, a squat rectangle with windows glowing yellow. It was gray too. What genius would paint a school gray? They just needed bars on the windows to complete the prison effect.

A movement caught my eye at the corner of the building. Someone was leaving the school and walking across the field toward the parking lot. It was a slim figure, a girl, in a red sweater with the hood up against the wind. She was leaning into it, and it looked like the sky was pushing down on her shoulders. She was surrounded by hundreds of people in both schools, and in the houses around the schools, but out on that field, she was totally alone.

Like the kid in the forest. If you didn't realize you were in a forest, lost, you wouldn't be afraid.

The figure got smaller as she got farther away.

But what if you know you're in the forest, and you know there's something that lives there? Something hairy, with big teeth. You can't see it, but you know it's there.

I heard Mrs. Stang moving on to the next topic. "Take out your textbooks, please." I fished a practice sheet from the pile. "You'll need your protractors."

Then, what if you hear the beast, hear its jaws, the snapping of a bone? Maybe you get a whiff of it, and it smells like something dead.

I took another look out the window. The figure was gone, all that remained was a mess of wrappers swirling on the wind.

Then you see its eyes, glowing red, watching you.

"Gavin, please take your seat."

I searched the field, wanting one last look at the figure in the hood.

Of course, if you don't believe the beast exists, then the snapping noise is just a twig, and the smell is fallen leaves, and the glowing red is a sunset. And you're not afraid at all.

A bit of eraser bounced off the glass by my elbow. I turned to the class. Trist was gesturing toward Mrs. Stang, who had set her hands firmly on her hips.

"If we're all ready now, we could begin."

Alexis snickered behind her hands.

I slipped in behind my desk.

"What were you looking at?" Trist whispered.

"Nothing, really." I dug in my pack for the protractor. "For a minute I thought it was someone I knew."

I glanced back over my shoulder at the window. In the parking lot at the top of the field a set of tail-lights was leaving, tail-lights on a blue sports car.

Fourteen

[14]

I stood on the back step, zipping my jacket collar right up under my chin. The morning grass was brittle with frost and the air was crisp. The sky was the brilliant blue of Jasey McVeigh's eyes. My breath puffed out in clouds.

It's funny what you remember. Like the sound my shoes made on the grass, a fragile kind of crunch, like stepping on the thinnest glass, as I crossed the lawn to the shed. And then a complete absence of sound as I stood stupidly looking at the shed door.

It was open just a crack, just the smallest bit to tell me that someone had been in there. The hairs on my neck prickled and, despite the coldness of the morning, dampness spread under my arms. My bike was gone. I knew without even looking.

I always locked my bike inside the shed. Always. And I always pulled the door closed. Always. The only other stuff in the shed, the lawn mower, rakes, no one else used. No one else went into the shed. But someone had been in there.

I let my pack drop to the grass. With my breath stuck in my chest, I slid open the door. Where my bike should have been, there was an enormous gaping emptiness. My helmet lay on the dirt floor like an egg pushed out of the nest. Dad's bolt cutters were in the dirt beside it.

Funny what you think. I picked up the bolt cutters, knowing Dad would be some ticked to see them laying on the ground. I wouldn't want Dad to be ticked. He doesn't keep his tools in the shed. Says they'll rust. He keeps them in the basement on a pegboard, each one outlined in black marker, over his workbench.

In the basement. My breath came raggedly, like I'd been running three times around the school field. In the basement, where only me or Mom or Dad could have got them. Or Blake.

There was nothing I had ever owned that Blake didn't at one time or another claim. My Halloween candy would be gone weeks before Trist's because Blake ravaged it. I don't mean just snagging the occasional chocolate bar. I mean taking it by the handful. He even took the stuff he didn't like, spitting it out in front of me. When I was first saving up for my bike, I made the mistake of keeping the money under my mattress. He found it and took it. Denied it. I opened a bank account then. At supper he'll eat the meat off my plate like it belongs to him, just reaching over and stabbing it with his fork when no one is looking. And I'd almost rather not get good stuff for my birthday, because it bugs me more when he breaks it or steals it.

If he really needed something of mine, it would be different. Like a kidney. Who would turn down their brother for something that could save his life? Even a brother like Blake. I'd give him the kidney, or blood, or bone marrow. I would. But I bet he'd rather die than take it from me.

For Christmas once, Mom bought me a little wooden totem pole. She wrapped it with tissue paper so it wouldn't break and set it in a blue box. It was hand-painted, with a frog and killer whale, and, on top, a blue raven. The way the raven perched, his head forward, his eyes bright, it made me feel good to look at it. It was a hopeful-looking raven. I set it on the shelf over my bed so I could look at it before I went to sleep.

I woke up the next morning to find Blake in my room. He was still in his pajamas. He was standing by my bed, looking at the totem pole. He saw me watching him, and he took the totem pole and, right there in front of me, snapped it in two.

I crossed the lawn in three strides and slammed through the kitchen door.

"What did you do with my bike?"

Blake was still at the table. I launched myself at him, hating him with every bit of my being.

"You took it, I know you did!" I screamed the words. Dad wasn't home yet. Mom was standing at the counter looking stunned. I didn't care if the whole world heard me. He was sitting there chewing his toast, smirking at me. I grabbed him by the shirt.

"I never took your stinking bike." He knocked my hands away.

"You did too! You used Dad's bolt cutters from the basement. What did you do with it?" I clawed at him.

Mom threw herself between Blake and me. "Blake, you didn't take his bike." She made it a statement, like, "Say it isn't so."

He stood up from the table, turning to her with barely veiled disgust. "What's it to you?"

She backed off a step. Her voice was quiet. "Just go on to school, Gavin. You'll have to walk. We'll get this all straightened out."

"I'm not going until he tells me what he did with my bike!" I struggled not to cry. Who would straighten it out? Not Mom, that was for sure.

Blake flipped me the finger.

"You're an ass—"

Mom held out her hand to stop me. "No swearing!"

Blake imitated her. "No swearing!" Then he hurled a string of foul words. I lunged for him. I wanted to have his eyeballs in my hands, just like the cow eyeball. I wanted to break his leg bones. I wanted to tear his heart out of his chest.

With one hand he threw me, sending me crashing into the counter. My head hit first. My vision clouded to gray, then black, then every color in the rainbow.

Mom bent down on one knee beside me. "Oh, baby." Her face creased with concern. "When is all this going to stop?" She put her hand on my head, feeling for a lump. The way she sucked in her breath made it clear she'd found a good one. Her hands felt so cool on my face. And they smelled nice, like lotion. I wanted to pull her arms around me, have her hold me like she used to, have her stop the insanity that surrounded and engulfed us. I wanted her to rescue me.

Blake watched. For an instant the fire faded from his eyes and I thought he was going to go, that it was over. But I was wrong. And that was the mistake I made, thinking that anger fueled my brother's attacks. Because it wasn't anger. Not that day. It was cold, cruel fear. If I'd known that then, maybe I could have stopped him. But his face turned to slate, and his fists tightened at his sides. He grabbed Mom by the arm, yanking her to her feet, his face just inches from hers. Then he spit in her face.

She hit him. It was a feeble slap to his face, but it may as well have been a bomb. He took her by both shoulders and shook her, shook her so hard that her head snapped back and forth. I struggled to my feet.

Up until the time with the broom, my mother had never hit either one of us, not even spanked us. Dad has sent us both to the emergency room, but Mom never laid a hand on us. Her neck was making ugly crackling sounds. Her eyes were white, just white, because the force of his shaking made the rest roll away.

My stomach liquefied and I swallowed the panic that jammed up in my throat. A voice in my head was poking at me. *"Call the police. He's lost it completely and you're going to need help."* The phone was two steps away on the wall. *"Three numbers. 9. 1. 1. That's all. Get the phone."* But it's funny what you think. I thought Dad wouldn't want the police at his door. That he'd have to go to the police station and he wouldn't get his sleep. That they might take Mom away in an ambulance. And if they took her away, maybe she'd never come back. It would be just them and me. Alone. That was more frightening than anything. I forced myself to breathe, the blood pounding through the side of my head where I'd hit the counter. I sucked in a huge breath. Then, with a scream that tore itself out of my throat, I flung myself at Blake.

His face was a grinning madman's. I plunged my fists into his stomach and pushed him as hard as I could away from Mom. He stumbled back. Mom fell away. I could hear her crying behind me. Again and again I pummeled Blake's stomach, driving my fists deep with every punch, feeding on his grunts of pain. Again and again and again. Then his hands came down on my head.

At first they just kind of rested there, like an evil benediction. I shot a fist up under his ribs. The hands on my head tightened. I sent my left fist into his side. It was crazy what I was feeling, that I could beat him, that I could win. My muscles were strong; my shoulders felt loose and warm, like a boxer's. I drew back my right hand, the nails digging into my palm, ready to hit him again, when I felt a clump of hair loosen on my scalp. Then his knee came up into my nose.

It hurt so bad I thought I should see God. The pain nail-gunned right between my eyes, then ringed my head, driving spikes through my skull. He kneed me again. I spewed corn flakes on his shoes. A third time he kneed me, and my legs went out from under me, and the pain went away, and I hung off his hands until he dropped me into my own pool of puke.

The last thing I remember is the sound of breaking glass as Mom broke the coffee pot over Blake's head.

FIFTEEN

[15]

It was beyond stitches, of course. The doctor bandaged my nose and said I'd need surgery if I wanted to breathe through more than one nostril again, but that he couldn't do anything for the shape of it. I would just have to get used to that.

Trist said it made me look tough. Marc said I looked like a raccoon. Ms. Priestly gasped, the scalp between her hair worms turning bright red. "Who did this to you?"

I told her. My front tooth was loose too, and my lips all swollen, so I slurred my words a bit.

"That young man needs to be dealt with." She stormed to the classroom phone and punched in some numbers.

"Isn't there some kind of penal colony for guys like Blake?" Trist chalked a hangman's noose on the board.

"A penile colony?" Troy slapped Marc on the back. "You mean for dorks?"

"Blake is beyond dorkdom. He's not even human. He's, he's, excretion." Trist drew a steaming pile under the noose.

"Take your seats." Ms. Priestly clomped to the front of the class. Trist wiped the drawings off the board with his sleeve. "At least in this classroom we can all rely on order." She snapped open an English text and lectured like the whole world depended on it.

I was beginning to regret saying it was Blake. The way people were reacting, so angry, it was like I'd done this to myself. I should have told them what Dad told me to, that I'd fallen down the stairs.

A strange car was parked at the house when I got home, a nice car, with plush gray upholstery. When I went in, a man in a suit was sitting on the couch, and a woman in a suit was perched on the edge of a chair. Dad was in his undershirt and pants, unshaven, his hair pushed up at the back where he'd been sleeping on it. Mom was wearing a clean robe. The woman's eyes got really big when she saw my face.

"You must be Gavin." She got up to greet me. She was young, with nice red lips. She stretched her face into a big smile.

I smiled back at her. My front tooth was bleeding a bit, and her smile faded from her face. She extended her hand and I shook it. It felt smooth and light, and very soft.

"We were just leaving." The man in the suit stood up, shaking my hand too.

My eyes fell to the woman's suit front. The tiniest bit of white lace peeped out between the lapels of her dark blue jacket.

"Thanks for keeping us abreast of this situation," the man said to my father.

I turned bright red. It hurt to blush, and my eyes started to water.

The woman's fine white brow crinkled with concern. "Oh, you poor dear boy."

I was afraid she was going to hug me. I stepped backwards, stumbled on the footstool, and backed into Dad. He put his hands on my shoulders, squeezing really hard.

"A little clumsy, this one."

The man and woman left. She glanced back up to the house and saw me watching, and gave me a little wave. I thought about blowing a kiss, but just waved back.

When I turned from the window, my dad's steel-eyed glare met me not two feet from my face. "What possessed you to talk about this to your teacher!" He stepped a foot closer. "Do you think I like our dirt out where everyone can see it?" He jabbed a thick finger at my chest. "Like we don't have enough problems without having suits poking their noses in where they don't belong!"

The image of the woman's suit came unbidden to my mind.

"Are you listening to me!"

I nodded, fast. My stomach was doing a slow cartwheel and I felt like I needed to sit down.

"Don't you ever, ever, talk about your brother. With anyone. Do you understand?"

I nodded. His breath stunk of old garlic.

"Look at you. You look like you're retarded or something, your nose flattened all over your face. All because of a bicycle. A stupid bike." He jabbed me once more with his finger for good measure, then slammed into his bedroom.

Did he really believe this was because of my bike?

Mom dabbed at her eyes with a tissue, her voice heaving. "They think we should send him away. To a boarding school, Gavin." She waved a pamphlet in front of my face. Woodman's Residential School. There was a picture of a boy in a striped necktie. I thought about Trist's hangman's noose. "Somewhere in the middle of Sask … Sask …"

"Saskatchewan?"

"Yes." She blew her nose with a honk. "The social worker said they have a very good success rate turning kids around if they get them soon enough. Before they're in real trouble with the law."

I wanted to say that maybe it was a bit late for that, but I left it alone.

"They stay a whole year, and don't even come home for holidays." She balled up the tissue over her eyes. "Not even for his birthday!" A low wail emerged from under the tissue.

I tried not to smile. A whole year. Maybe they would starve him, and he'd shrivel up like an old orange. I could lift weights and work out. By the time he got back, I might be as big as him.

"I know he's a handful. But he's not a bad person."

I rolled my eyes. No, Blake's not a bad person. He just permanently rearranged my face.

Maybe I'd get his room.

"They even pay for it. A subsidized program. Crime Prevention, or something."

I held the pamphlet to my chest like a winning lottery ticket.

She stuffed the tissue into the pocket of her robe and snagged a new one from the box by the TV. "No. He's my son, and somehow or other, I'll figure out a way to make him mind." She dried her eyes, blew her nose, jammed the tissue in her pocket, and tightened the belt of the robe. "After all, we're a family."

I tossed the pamphlet onto the TV and plunked down on the couch, a sigh whistling out of me. Nothing was easy with my mother. Nothing made sense in this family. And nothing but being blood kept us under the same roof. Very bad blood.

"You never told Dad that Blake was hurting you, did you?"

She didn't answer. She'd already left the room.

SIXTEEN

[16]

"Jelly donut or fritter?" Mrs. McVeigh held the donut box out to me.

"Jelly." I wiggled it in front of Grandpa Jack. "Squeak squeak."

Jasey's seat was empty tonight—again—even though she was at home. She was grounded. She'd appeared only once, wearing her running tights and a sweatshirt. She'd barely glanced at us, just grabbed a Coke from the fridge then stalked off.

"You not playing?" I called after her. She didn't answer.

If she even noticed the white tape over my nose, she didn't say anything. I had hoped for some sympathy, that maybe she'd stand really close to me and hold my face in her hands, and gently, oh so softly, kiss it all better.

Mrs. McVeigh and Gran threw themselves into a flutter when they saw me, sitting me down and stroking my head, cluck clucking and tsk tsking. Grandpa Jack took one look and a dark cloud covered his face.

"Your brother?" he asked.

I nodded.

He just shook his head.

I bit into the donut, letting the soft filling squish into my mouth.

"I hope you're all prepared for defeat," Grandpa Jack said, rubbing his hands together.

"You can't rely on pure luck. Luck is finite." Trist handed him the dice. "Roll to see who goes first."

As we played I could hear the TV in the other room. Jasey was flipping channels. Her being so close, but not with us, distracted me. "Are you going to roll?" Trist shoved the dice at me. Mrs. McVeigh touched him lightly on the arm.

I shook the dice. "Six. That puts me on Park Place. I guess I'll buy that."

Grandpa Jack groaned. "I guess you would."

Mrs. McVeigh handed me the blue card. I tucked it under the game board in front of me.

Gran got the first railroad. Mrs. McVeigh bought up all the orange properties. Trist landed in jail.

"Off to a roaring start."

I'd have to land on Boardwalk if I stood a chance at winning the game. I collected my $200 for passing Go and landed on Chance. I was in jail with Trist.

Grandpa Jack beat me to Boardwalk. "I'll buy that." He handed over his money and smiled at me. "Looks like we'll be partners."

I looked at the small pile of money left in front of him. Neither one of us had enough to buy the other out. I reached across to shake his hand. "Partners."

Having the prime properties didn't assure us of the win. Trist and his mother teamed up in a formidable alliance with one entire side of the board to their credit. Gran was wiped out early on.

"I'll make us some popcorn. May as well. Not like I have anything else to do." She called to the other room. "Jasey, would you like some popcorn?"

There was no answer. The volume on the TV notched up.

"That girl knows I watch the news at 10:00, right?" Grandpa Jack was counting out a large wad of cash to pay for two hotels.

Gran shot him a look. "Of course she knows. Leave her be."

The TV snapped off. I watched the doorway, hoping Jasey would come in. Grandpa Jack rolled for us.

He groaned. "Luxury tax. Help me add it up, Gavin."

Trist grinned. We were heading into their side of the board. I took a pile of money and counted it out.

"You count that properly?" Grandpa Jack took

the pile from me and counted it again. There was a sound of feet going upstairs. Jasey was retreating.

Gran stood at the sink watching the game. Upstairs, water was running.

Mrs. McVeigh said, "I think he can count."

"I know he can. Just roll, why don't you?"

They landed on a railroad, their own. The water upstairs stopped. Was she going to bed already? Wasn't she even going to say good night?

A bill slipped from my hands and under the table, and I stooped down to get it. It was lying right by Grandpa Jack's foot. He wore gray socks, and I could see the edge of a red stripe just below his pant leg. They were the same socks Trist wore. Maybe Gran bought both Trist and Grandpa Jack their socks. I was just about to grab the bill when I noticed his foot. It was twitchin—random shifting little movements that weren't connected to anything else. I'd seen him move like this before but hadn't thought anything about it. I watched, mesmerized. It didn't stop.

I was four when I first started coming here, back when Gran used to babysit me. Uncle Pat was here then, occupying a chair in the living room, spending much of his day watching TV. He didn't seem to care what he watched, or at least he didn't say anything, so we'd watch kids' shows together. I'd sit on the floor right by his chair, and all through the show his feet would twitch in this exact same way.

"What are you doing down there so long?" Grandpa Jack was losing his patience.

I brought my head up so fast I bonked it on the table. The others were dealing money back and forth, rolling the dice. I sat there rubbing my head, looking at him.

"Gavin, are you all right?" Mrs. McVeigh's forehead creased into lines.

"You look like Vanessa did the day we did the eyeball," Trist said.

Grandpa Jack checked his watch. "He's fine. Just roll."

"It's all this bickering. No one is themselves tonight." Mrs. McVeigh patted my arm.

"I'm all right. I just hit my head a bit, that's all."

Grandpa Jack took the dice. "I'll roll for us." He laughed. "We have this game in the bag."

I stared at Grandpa Jack, I know I did. I searched his face for any signs of crookedness. I watched to see if he lurched at all in his chair.

A victory whoop lifted from the other side of the table. We'd landed on their property.

"We're wiped out. Finito." Grandpa Jack threw in our cards.

Trist high-fived his mother.

I'd seen his hands shake. And the way he'd fidgeted at the movie—everything in my stomach inverted.

"Jasey," Gran said. "Did you come down for some popcorn?"

I looked up. Jasey was leaning in the doorway, watching me. She'd seen me staring at Grandpa Jack. Her bright blue eyes had narrowed, her eyebrows creased just like her mother's. At first I thought she was looking at my nose, and that's why she was so upset. But it was more than that. She had seen something in my face, something that revealed my discovery about Grandpa Jack. She knew that I knew. And if I knew he had it, then she could no longer foster the smallest doubts. She knew he had the disease too.

"No, Gran. I just came down for my book." Pulling her eyes away from me, she retrieved a paperback from the table. The color was gone from her skin, and her hands holding the book trembled. She bent beside Grandpa Jack and kissed him on the cheek.

He closed his eyes and, with a gentle hand, held her cheek against his.

"That's my girl."

SEVENTEEN

[17]

"What do you call what Uncle Pat has?" I asked Gran. I was waiting for Trist to get ready for school. I walked, he rode, then when we were out of sight of the house he'd double me to school. I studied Gran's face carefully, watching for any sign that she knew about Grandpa Jack.

She turned from the sandwich she was wrapping. "Huntington's disease. It's kind of like Alzheimer's in the way it scrambles the brain, but HD is genetic. And it affects speech and movement."

"But you don't always get it, if it's in the family?"

She looked at me hard. "No. If a parent has it, then each child has a fifty-fifty chance of inheriting it. But only if the parent has the gene."

Uncle Pat had never married or had children. But Grandpa Jack had had Sam. And Sam had had Trist and Jasey. I swallowed hard.

"How do you know if you're going to get it?"

"You don't, not unless you're tested, or until you start showing symptoms. Although sometimes people get depressed, maybe make mistakes, years before they start to have any big symptoms. I don't think Pat did, though."

"So he didn't know he was going to get it?"

Gran shook her head. "He already had symptoms before the test was developed."

"So Trist could have a test?" And Jasey?

"Well, when he's of age. But he's not going to get the disease."

I could hear Trist thumping down the stairs. "Because his dad had the test?"

"No, dear. Because Grandpa Jack doesn't have the disease. And since he doesn't, then neither would Trist's father. Or his kids."

She sounded so totally sure. In Gran's mind, the hairy thing with big teeth didn't exist in this house. How could she not see it? I envied her blindness.

"Did Grandpa Jack have the test?" I tried to keep my voice from revealing the panic that I was feeling.

"No. But never mind Grandpa Jack. He's almost seventy. It's almost unheard of to get it this late. He's going to die of being old and grumpy. Nothing more than that."

"What's this about Grandpa Jack?" Trist stood in the doorway, still in his pajamas.

"Trist, you're going to be late!" Gran swiveled her head to check the clock.

"I'm not going. I phoned Mom. She said I could stay home."

Gran's hand darted for his forehead, but he brushed her away. "I'm sick."

He looked fine to me. "What've you got? The flu?"

"What difference does it make?"

"Well then, you better get off to bed." Gran slid the lunch bag into the fridge. "And you better get off to school." She swept me toward the door.

"You're not really sick, are you?" I tried to make it sound joking, but his mouth set in a hard line and he stalked off.

My illustration of the boy in the book put him somewhere between a POW and a skeleton. If he didn't soon get rescued I'd have to draw him as a stick figure.

"He's changed." Ms. Priestly leaned over my shoulder. "I don't know what it is. It's like he's haunted."

I shaded some gray in the hollows of his cheeks. "Where he's at, it's not exactly summer camp."

She looked at me for a moment. "It's more than that. There's pain underneath the drawing." She paused, looked at the picture, then again at me. "It's like you know who this boy is."

"Maybe. I guess the author's done his job then."

"The artist too." She rested her hands on my shoulders for an instant before leaving me to my work.

If I were sure no one would see, I'd sketch Jasey into the picture, a wild-haired Jasey, barefoot, with animal-skin clothing and a necklace of feathers at her throat. She would have been born in the forest, immune to its loneliness.

"What is lonely?" she'd say, in her attempt to understand the language of the boy. Because if you've always been alone, you wouldn't know any different. She'd be perfectly happy in the forest, and with her, the boy would be happy too.

With pencil strokes as fine as gossamer, I drew her in the trees: tall and strong, at home. She was smiling. No one would see her. Only I would know she was there. Maybe she is there, watching the boy, laughing at his foolish attempts to catch fish, to survive. Maybe she breathes, like a whisper on the wind, what he needs to know. Maybe she dances in his firelight after he falls asleep.

I dampened my brush, then touched the bristles with red the color of my hair. Lightly, so that you'd only see it if you were looking for it, I dabbed the paint into the boy's hair.

The library was quiet, just a few students at the tables. I picked a terminal away from the others and called up the Internet.

Huntington's disease. An inherited brain disorder. Progressive deterioration. Severe incapacitation. Death. Usually appears between the ages of thirty and forty-five, but can appear as early as age two, as late as seventy. Involuntary movement, slurred speech, cognitive impairment, personality changes. I kept a dictionary beside me but didn't bother to use it. Even without knowing what all the words meant, the message was clear. If you carry the gene you will develop the disease. If you live long enough.

Trist and Jasey's father killed himself. Looking into a future with this kind of disease might cause someone to commit suicide. But if that was the case, did he see the disease in his father so many years before anyone else? Or did he see it in himself?

I walked toward home, the streets empty, the light already fading. Before it was Huntington's disease, people used to call it St. Vitus Dance, because of the movement. I thought of Jasey, her long legs on the running track, her smooth gait, the even strides, the absolute strength. She didn't run anymore. The disease had already marked her, even if she never got it. And Trist was its next victim.

Eighteen

[18]

Trist was in the kitchen, making a mess in the blender with a banana and ice cubes. He didn't see me come in. "Feeling better?" I jabbed him in the ribs.

"Jeez Louise! Don't you ever knock?"

He didn't look very sick. He was dressed, his hair was combed, and judging by the ketchup stains on his T-shirt, he'd been eating pretty well. "So why were you faking?"

He shot me a look. "You want some of this?"

I looked into the blender jar. A slime of brown stuff coated the glass. "I don't think so." I watched with disgust as he gulped the lumps.

He set the jar down and looked at me like he was considering whether he should tell me something. He upended the jar, letting the brown sludge splat into the sink.

"Jasey woke me up last night, going out her window. She came home just as it was getting light."

I felt the breath stop in my lungs.

"All night. I know, because I stayed awake, waiting. When she finally got home she didn't even bother going through her window. She came right in the door. Said she was just coming in from a run." He set the glass in the sink.

My brain felt like the brown stuff in the blender. Where could she possibly be going in the middle of the night?

"Did you say anything to her about it?"

He looked away. "Yeah, I said something. And so did she. She said I was just a kid and that I should mind my own business. That she hated spies. And then she said if I told anyone, the next time she left she'd never come back."

My tongue stuck to the roof of my mouth. "Did you tell anyone?"

"I just told you, you jerk."

"Anyone who counts? Does your mom know?"

"No. As far as Mom knows, she has Jasey under control. Jasey makes a big show of studying after supper and going to bed early. Mom sits back, like her work is done. Then Jasey climbs out her window." He shook his head slowly back and forth. "Mom doesn't have any control over Jasey. I don't think she would even if she knew. Jasey is way beyond control." He sighed. "It's like something is eating her alive."

The hairy thing. It has its teeth in her. I hated what I had to tell Trist, hated what I knew.

"Jasey's right about your grandfather, Trist. He does have Huntington's disease."

Trist's breathing grew quiet, his eyes narrowing on mine. "You're lying."

I shook my head. "I saw, Trist. He moves just like your Great Uncle Pat did at the beginning. He's forgetting things and dropping things and I'm sorry, but I don't know how you can't see it for yourself. He's got it! Your grandpa has the disease."

"Gran doesn't think so and you'd think she'd know." His voice was sarcastic, defiant.

I shrugged. "Maybe she doesn't know. Or doesn't want to know yet. But that doesn't change it."

"Who made you the expert on my family?"

"I don't blame you for not wanting to believe this. It's a terrible disease, and now it's breathing down your neck …"

"Shut up! You don't know anything! What are you, some doctor or something? That's really funny. Like Dr. Idiot, more like."

I swallowed hard on that. "But maybe your dad didn't have it …"

"Leave him out of this."

"But even if he did …"

"What part of shut up don't you get! He didn't

have it. Grandpa Jack doesn't have it. I'm never going to get it. I'm never going to crap in my pants or drool my food or lose my freaking mind. It isn't going to happen. Because Grandpa Jack doesn't have it!"

He turned away from me and I could tell he was crying.

"You want me to go home?"

He was quiet for a long time. But then he turned around. His eyes were red, but more than that, they were angry. I'd never seen him so angry. When he spoke, his words were like ice.

"You're an idiot. And you're wrong. But if you breathe a word of this to anyone, I'll kill you."

NINETEEN

[19]

I heard Mom sobbing as I opened the back door. It was quiet and contained, punctuated with nose blowing.

Mom had been a little strange since she broke the coffee pot over Blake's head. She cleaned out way back in the fridge, put new paper on the cupboard shelves, even cleaned out his bedroom, washed the walls and carpet, opened the windows to air it out. It was like she was releasing something from the house.

She was sitting at the kitchen table, and I blinked my eyes a couple of times when I saw her, because she was fully dressed. And not just jeans and a sweatshirt, but real clothes, and pantyhose! Her hair was done and she had makeup on, and for a minute, I thought I was eight years old again.

"Oh, Gavin, I'm sorry. I'm just a mess." She honked into a tissue and dabbed streaks of mascara from under her eyes.

I looked around for evidence of the social workers

having been—cups and saucers, a plate of cookies—but there was nothing. Dad was snoring behind his bedroom door. Blake didn't appear to be around. "Who died?"

"What?" She looked at me, her red eyes confused. "Oh, you mean these." She motioned to her clothes. She tossed a section of the newspaper at me, the classified ads. One was circled with red marker. "Wanted: Zoo Assistant. Experience an asset." There was an address, then "Apply in person."

Mom was wearing her best suit, pale blue wool that with her fair hair made her look like a summer day. On her feet she wore a tiny pair of shiny black pumps.

"Ah, zoo assistant?" I couldn't keep the smile from creeping across my face. Experience with animals? Blake qualified as an animal, as did my father.

"It's close to home. And I like animals."

"Sure you do. So why are you crying?"

She hiccuped a huge sob. "I didn't get the job." Her shoulders heaved with a resigned sigh.

Now there's a surprise. Maybe they were looking for someone with, I don't know, rubber boots?

"I didn't know you were looking for work." I liked the idea of Mom working. I liked the idea of her wearing real clothes instead of a bathrobe. Somehow that lent normalcy to our family.

"Just a part-time job. Just to get out of the house."

"Maybe you could get a job doing what you used to do. Before the accident." What did she do? I was trying to remember.

"Oh no. I'll never work in publishing again. All those anxious writers. They make me nervous."

I scanned the paper. "Here, look at this one. And it's close enough to walk."

She read the ad. "Happy Times Dry Cleaners. Laundry presser. Flexible hours. Must be able to stand heat. Call for interview." She looked at me. "It's perfect!" She reached for the phone.

She was back in her robe by suppertime, but she was humming to herself, snapping a handful of spaghetti into a pot. "Scrape some carrots for us, will you Gavin?"

I peeled long orange strips off the carrots into the sink. She worked beside me, brushing mushrooms.

"You're not putting those right in the sauce, are you?" I hate mushrooms—so slippery, and all those spore things.

She plunked them into the pot. "Everyone likes mushrooms."

I sighed. "Mom, do think maybe if this job works out, you'd ever consider leaving Dad?"

Her hands dropped in the sink like stones and I

felt her eyes piercing the side of my head. "Why would you say a thing like that?"

My ears flushed red. So that we could run off and live by ourselves. You could iron clothes all day; I could go to art school. You could put mushrooms on the side. "I don't know. I just thought maybe Dad was a little hard on you."

"Oh, Gavin." She rested a wet hand on my shoulder. "Your father loves me." She went back to cleaning the mushrooms. "He's under so much pressure at work, what with the new dogs and all those urine tests for drugs and alcohol. He has a temper." She shook her brush at me. "But he's never once hurt me. You remember that. Your father loves me. He didn't have much of a childhood, but he's a good man. Deep down, he's a really good man."

How deep would you have to dig to find a shred of good?

"His parents died when he was really young, right?"

Mom turned, suddenly intent on the mushrooms. Her voice was quiet. "That's what we always told you." She scrubbed frantically. "But they're both still alive."

"I have grandparents I don't even know about?"

She shushed me, then said, "You wouldn't want to know them. And I would never allow it. He's a monster of a man, spent half his adult life in prison for assault crimes. And your grandmother isn't much better. She used to put your dad's hand on the stove burner when he misbehaved." Her hands paused, and she wiped away new tears. "They used to keep him locked in a closet while they went out drinking. For days, Gavin. Sometimes he'd be in there for days."

We didn't have one picture in the house of Dad as a child. Now I knew why. He'd erased that part of his life so that it didn't exist anymore.

Except in us, his own children.

Trist told me this story about fleas, about how if we could jump like fleas, we could clear a high-rise. But circus fleas are put in jars, and when they jump, they hit their heads on the lid. So they learn to jump only just to the height of the lid. Then, when they have babies, the babies only jump that high too, even out of the jar, because that's all they've seen. They don't know that they can jump higher.

"Your dad does the best he can. I'm not saying I agree with everything he does, or that it's okay. But he's known hell." She tossed the rest of the mushrooms into the pot. "Don't ever tell him that I told you."

TWENTY

I was around the side of the house before I saw them—Blake and his friends, draped on the back porch, smoking. Clay was sitting on the railing. They were talking, but stopped when they saw me. It was too late to turn around now.

"Well," Clay whistled long and low. "Look at the Technicolor kid."

My face was still blue between my eyes and yellow everywhere else from the bruising. It looked like one of those topographical maps with the different colors showing different elevations.

Clay turned to Blake. "Your old man do that to him?" There was a hint of anger in his voice.

Blake avoided Clay's stare. "Who cares?"

Clay jumped down from the railing. "Maybe I do."

Blake shot me an evil look and jammed his hands in his pockets.

Clay wore a black leather jacket that fell to his

hips, and jeans, the expensive kind. His blond hair was longer than the other guys', precision cut and sleek. Hair like that didn't come out of a barber shop. His thin face was plastered with zits, but even so, he looked good. He approached me, and I marveled at the sharpness of his eyes. They were brown, but light, almost gold. They were the eyes of an animal.

He held me by the chin. "Who did this to you." It wasn't a question, but a demand.

I swallowed. I flicked my eyes to Blake. "He did."

Clay examined my nose for a long time, not saying anything. With a long thin finger he tapped the end of it. "That hurt?"

I jerked back from him. The guys laughed. "Your nose would too if you were picking cartilage out of it." I smacked his hand out of my face.

The crowd of guys got very quiet. Blake smirked. A shade of color crossed Clay's cheeks, then he smiled. With an easy grace he turned to Blake. Blake's smirk disappeared.

"Your little brother must have really pissed you off." Clay slipped a pack of smokes from his jacket pocket and, without looking from Blake, offered them to me.

I shook my head. He held them there, clearly expecting me to take them. Finally I stuttered, "No, thanks."

He glanced back at me. "Smart kid. Don't start." He opened the pack and flipped a cigarette to his lips, lighting it with a click of a silver lighter. He drew the smoke deeply into his lungs as he turned back to Blake. He exhaled through his teeth.

"So what exactly did he do? Mess with your stamp collection?"

The guys laughed, but Blake met his stare unflinchingly. "I don't have a stamp collection."

"Maybe the kid took something that was yours. I could understand you getting bent if he took something. Like your action figures."

The guys laughed at this too. I squirmed. I hadn't played with action figures for at least two years. That's not counting the day last summer when Trist and I played with his, but only because it was raining all day and we were bored, and we were so embarrassed we swore each other to secrecy.

Blake pushed away from the railing, his eyes flashing. "It's none of your business."

Clay stepped closer to Blake. "Oh, but it is. Because someone who smashes a face for no reason is weak, a dangerous weakness to himself. And to his friends." Clay held his hands out to the side like a ceramic saint. "I wouldn't want to think you were that kind of guy."

He turned to me. "Blake ever gives you any trouble,

you call me." He rested his arm across my shoulders. Blake slouched back against the railing, his arms crossed.

"I could give you a little something for your nose, make you feel better." Clay reached into his pocket.

The guys pressed close. "Hand it around. Come on."

Clay waved them off. "Just for our young friend." He pulled out a packet of white powder, holding it in the inside of his hand. "This is fine. Uncut. Only the best."

I busted out in a sweat.

"Just a taste, Clay. Share it." Their faces were wide-eyed, hungry.

My mouth went completely dry.

"Like I just said, it's not for you." He pulled me tighter to him. "What's your name?"

I told him.

"Gavin. That's a sweet name." He held the packet in front of my eyes and the whiteness of it held me like a hypnotist's crystal. "The best friends are the ones no one suspects. The sweet ones. Innocent." He turned his hand slowly back and forth so the light on the package shone rainbows. "The ones no one sees."

With a long fingernail he slit the package. "Open your mouth."

My tongue was like cardboard and the words barely came out. "I don't want any."

"I'll have his. Let me have his." The faces were harder, desperate.

He studied me, his topaz eyes searching mine. "Gavin, you and I could be great friends." He wet the end of his finger and dipped it in the package. The white powder coated it like clear Kool-Aid crystals. He grinned, wide, like a chimp, and I pulled back from the grimace. Then he rubbed his finger on his gums.

"Very fine." He ran his tongue over his teeth, then again wet his finger and dipped into the packet.

"Open up."

I might have taken it, if I thought it would put my nose back in the right place. I know I would have taken it if it could have erased Blake out of my life. If it could make my parents normal. I shook my head.

His arm tightened on my shoulder. "We all have it in ourselves to be friends. All of us. Even if you think you don't, I know. I've seen it again and again. It's there in you, Gavin. Don't fool yourself. You're one of us." He released me, and I stumbled back.

"Here you are, boys. A little treat." Clay handed the packet to the eager hands. They fell on it like vultures, doling it out in silent greedy snorts. My head felt light, like it wasn't part of me anymore. I lurched for the kitchen door, hating how it tempted me, wanting to escape.

"You have it in you." Clay was watching me, a small smile on his pocked face. "You're smarter than him." He nodded at Blake.

Blake was hunched over the package, wiping the sides then licking his finger. He carefully tore the plastic and licked it clean, sucking it through his teeth. He looked different, the way his head hung forward, his shoulders stooped. It disgusted me. I yanked open the door.

Clay's voice followed me into the house. "With me, you can have whatever you need. Whatever you want is yours. You have it in you. Don't deny it. I know exactly who you are."

TWENTY-ONE

[20]

"We don't have the gene for this." Trist sat back from the sewing machine and stretched. We were in Textiles class learning how to bar tack an apron pocket. "It's not like we're ever going to use this stuff."

Alexis shot him a look over her machine. "Chromosome, you mean. Some of the finest fashion designers are men."

"Like I said, we don't have the gene."

She rolled her eyes, feeding a square of cotton under the needle of her machine. "My uncle knits."

"Oh, now there's a life skill they should teach us. Knitting. Then we could knit our own blankets. And long underwear." Trist jammed his apron pocket through the machine.

"He knits sweaters. They're quite beautiful. My mother has one with cables and patterns. It must have taken him months to do it."

"Maybe he's in jail. Lots of time on his hands."

"I heard that."

My apron pocket puckered into a snarl of stitches and I swore softly.

"I heard that too."

Roger's apron was shaping up nicely, owing, no doubt, to the fact that he actually measured his fabric pieces. His foot pumped the pedal and the fabric charged forward.

"Why do you have poodles on your apron?" Trist was picking out stitches too, and we both looked enviously at Roger's almost finished project.

"It's for my mother. She loves poodles. We have two of them."

"Toy?" Alexis asked.

"As in stuffed?"

"As in their breed." She rolled her eyes at Trist's ignorance.

"What purpose on this planet does a tiny poodle serve?" Trist sneered. His dog Barkley was as mixed as a dog could be, stone deaf now, with really smelly breath. "They can't fetch a stick or a ball. And they're hardly guard dogs."

"They're good company. They sleep on my mother's bed."

Bunny sleeps up on the bed with my dad too. He gave me the job of walking her after school and that's where I find her, curled up next to him on the pillow.

I hadn't wanted to walk her at first. Dad showed me the commands, how to use my voice and the lead. "See? Look at how she falls into step beside you." He clapped his arm around my shoulder. "I told you she liked you! You're not so stupid with dogs."

Thanks, Dad.

"And don't forget these." He tossed me a box of super-size plastic bags. "You'll need two or three."

Oh, good.

Walking Bunny makes me all but disappear. People take one look at her striped haunches, her big barrel chest, and they get all bug-eyed and pale. They can't look away from the dog, like if they do she'll sink her teeth into them.

Not much for teeth, Bunny—she's like an unloaded gun. And she'd only attack if I commanded her to. Even if she had good teeth, it's not the dog they should be afraid of. They should be afraid of me.

Trist leveled a disdainful look at Roger. "Your poodles probably have a litter box."

"They're still dogs, Trist. They're just small." Roger's voice was shaking.

"They're just snacks, more like. Barkley would love your poodles." Trist smacked his lips.

Roger became very intent on his apron.

"I mean, why would you have such puny dogs when you could have a real one?" Trist's tone was combative. He was looking for a fight.

"Leave him alone, Trist."

"No. In nature, dogs like that would never survive. And we breed them?"

"It's not like we live in a jungle or something," I said.

"Ooh, very sharp." Trist scowled at me. "What an astute observation."

Alexis watched me silently under her dark eyebrows. Roger glanced nervously from Trist, to me and then back to Trist.

"I know what that means. Astute. I'm not stupid, you know."

Trist snorted. "Oh no, not you. Not with the brains in your family."

"I wanted her to get a golden retriever but they're too big for our place," Roger said, wide-eyed.

"Yeah," Trist cracked, "and they were all out of Shih Tzu."

"Shit-zoo." Marc guffawed from across the room.

"Anything is better than a toy poodle. Even a Shih Tzu."

Roger shrugged and bent over the sewing machine.

Miss Naples, the Textiles teacher, looked up from Vanessa's apron, where she was showing her how to sew on the ties. I can never say Miss Naples' name without blushing. "Is everyone on task?"

We turned to our machines in an uncomfortable silence. Roger kept his head low over his work. Alexis complimented him on his apron and he managed a weak smile.

Trist muttered at his sewing. "Human beings are the only species to actually celebrate freaks of nature. Anything else eliminates them. That's why the planet is the mess it is today."

Dad had told me the real reason he brought Bunny home. He said Mr. Murphy was going to have her put down. His eyes got all misty when he told me, and I thought for a minute he was going to cry.

I avoided Trist's eyes. He was talking about more than dogs. He was talking about me, about Blake, for sure. And I had the worst feeling of all that he was talking about his grandfather.

TWENTY-TWO

[22]

Blake draped the jacket carefully over the back of his chair before hunkering over his breakfast.

"Where did this jacket come from?" Mom felt the sleeve, rubbing it between her fingers. "It's real leather!"

Blake snapped it away from her fingers. "Clay gave it to me. What's it to you?"

"You don't have to talk that way to me, young man."

Blake mocked her voice. "You don't have to talk that way to me, young man."

She ignored him. "It must have cost a fortune. That's quite a gift."

"Yeah. He's generous." Blake sucked back his milk in one gulp, then belched. "Not everyone is so tight they squeak."

"You've never done without."

"I could do without this right now." He pushed away from the table.

"You have your Anger Management course to-night."

He slammed the kitchen door so hard that a cup fell off its hook.

Over the next few days he showed up with bags and bags of stuff from the best stores: designer jeans, the newest sneakers, a fat gold chain to wear around his neck. He even smelled like money.

"Who is this Clay, anyway?" Mom studied him suspiciously.

"You wouldn't know him. Not like he lives in this dump of a neighborhood."

He tossed all his socks in the trash and filled his drawer with logo socks at ten bucks a pair. He got a haircut from a fancy salon. He even got a manicure.

"A manicure? I've never had a manicure." Mom stood with her hands on her hips.

He bought Dad cases of beer and sat with him on his night off and drank it. "That's my boy. What do those social worker busybodies know about nothing?"

Mom claimed his old sneakers for me, which were almost new and fit if I stuffed the ends with paper. "Where is all this money coming from?" Her forehead scrunched into familiar lines of worry.

Sweat prickled under my arms. "Maybe he got a job."

"Maybe."

I got all the bologna because he didn't want a lunch from home. He wore a new shirt every day for a week. I should have cared because I knew where he was getting the money—or enough to know that it was nothing good he was doing. But he was as happy as Blake ever gets and that meant life was as peaceful as it ever got, and that's why I didn't care.

Or that's what I told myself. I knew he used Clay's drugs. And now he seemed to be selling them, too. Kids two years younger than me were already using drugs, drugs they bought at recess right off the schoolyard. Maybe from Blake.

"What a surprise," Trist sneered when I told him what I suspected. I was walking to school; Trist was pedaling slow circles around me. "That bottom-feeder is exactly the dumb-ass for the job. Totally expendable."

I shuddered as I thought about Clay on the back step. He surely saw me as the same kind of dupe.

Trist continued. "But Blake is even dumber than most. He doesn't realize he's supposed to turn in the money."

Clay wasn't going to be too happy with my brother.

Trist's tone changed slightly, but it carried a similar animosity. "Jasey's wearing a ring now."

I stopped on the sidewalk, my mouth gaping stupidly.

"She had it on when she came down for breakfast, then slipped it off before anyone noticed and put it in her pocket. But I saw it."

I stumbled after him. "What do you mean a ring?"

"A ring." He threw me a "you idiot" look. "A little gold circle thing with sparkly jewels? Guys buy them, girls wear them?"

My breakfast rolled uncomfortably in my stomach. "Like a friendship ring, you mean?"

"Some friend. It's more flashy than the one my mom wears."

A sick sense of dread washed over me.

"So, she's been sneaking out her window to be with a guy?"

"What did you think she was doing in the middle of the night? Robbing convenience stores?"

Actually, compared to what I was thinking right then, that wasn't such a bad thought. Grasping for reason, I said, "She could have bought the ring herself. Or found it. My dad found a perfectly good Swiss army knife once just laying in the road."

Trist's voice was tight, angry. "Think about it for a minute. She's never said anything to anyone about this guy. He's never come over. Never even phones her that I know about. And she sneaks out at night to see him. Something tells me she doesn't want anyone knowing about her midnight boyfriend." Trist dropped his feet off the pedals and kicked a stone down the pavement. "Maybe he's a dirty old man who likes young girls. Maybe he's a vampire." He turned to me and paused, his face set with anger and disgust. "Or maybe he's such slime that she's ashamed to have anyone know."

Jasey wearing a ring. Some guy's ring. A knot tightened in my throat. What was she doing with that guy in the middle of the night?

Beside me, I felt Trist's stare. His expression hadn't changed. He was looking at me with the same disgust, and it lifted the hairs off my scalp to see him looking at me like that.

TWENTY-THREE

[23]

I tossed and turned in bed, cursing the drone of Blake's TV, cursing the relentless images of Jasey McVeigh, watching the clock as it crawled toward 3:00 a.m. That's how I knew what time it was.

At first I thought it was a garbage truck, the low-pitched rumble on the street in front of the house. Then I recognized it. It was Clay's car.

Blake would be heading out for one of his all-nighters. I listened for his footsteps coming up from his room, but except for his TV, the house was quiet.

The rumble continued past the house, then slowed to an idle.

Or maybe Clay was coming to collect all the stuff, the logo socks and new shoes. I smirked to myself. Of course, that would mean I'd have to give back Blake's old shoes. And he'd want all the bologna.

I waited for Clay to pound on the door. Nothing.

I lay in my bed, studying the quiet. It was the

kind of quiet where you know something is wrong. The rumbling idle of the car was too far away. It couldn't be parked in front of our house. One by one, the hairs lifted on my neck. It was parked down the street. In front of the McVeighs'.

I remembered and knew, all at once. The figure on the high school field. The one in the red sweater. The one all alone. It was Jasey.

I threw the blankets off the bed and leapt to the window. I could see the tail-lights of the car parked in front of Trist's house. In the glow of a street lamp I could see it was the same blue car that had swallowed up Jasey that day. I pulled on jeans and a sweater and ran from my room. I didn't care if I woke anyone as I pounded down the stairs and out the front door.

The cold sidewalk hammered my bare feet and the night air wanted to stop in my throat. My hands balled into fists at my sides as I raced toward the car.

First, I would kill him. Then I would tear his body apart. Then I would take his pimpled head and drop kick it on the frozen road until it looked like a smashed Halloween pumpkin.

I yanked open the passenger's door and blinked in the sudden brightness of the dome light. Clay watched me lazily from behind the wheel. A sly smile spread on his greasy face. There was no one beside him.

I stood still, gasping.

Clay leaned forward and took a pack of cigarettes from the dash, pulling one out. He snapped a lighter and lifted the flame to the cigarette. His eyes narrowed in the snake of smoke, then he laughed.

"Do I have a new recruit?"

"N-no," I stuttered, stupid in my shame. "I j-just thought …"

Clay shook his head, his face an ugly sneer. He set his arm on the headrest, then extended the cigarette into the back seat.

A hand reached forward to take it. It was Blake's hand. And curled up next to Blake was Jasey McVeigh.

TWENTY-FOUR

[24]

"Gavin, it's hardly dawn!" Gran said, as she rubbed sleep from her eyes. The kitchen in the McVeigh house was still dark. I hadn't been able to sleep since seeing Blake and Jasey in Clay's car hours before.

"I've just got to check some math homework with Trist." I shouldered past Gran before she could ask any questions.

Trist's door was closed, a stripe at the bottom still showing dark. I stepped quietly past his door to the end of the hall and Jasey's room. I paused only for a moment to quiet my banging heart, then opened her door.

It smelled of roses and sweat, her room did. A lamp on the night table was lit, casting the room in yellow-pink light. Jasey, still in her clothes, was asleep on the bed. I slipped in and closed the door.

I absorbed it all, the bureau heaped with girl jewelry and hair stuff, a pair of dirty socks lying on the rug, a drawer pulled partway out. Sweat prickled

131

under my arms. Clouds of filmy underwear spilled from the open drawer.

Her running clothes were in a pile on the floor. Maybe she'd worn them yesterday. Or last year. It was like her "before" life in this room—before she stopped playing Monopoly, before she climbed out her window, before Blake.

I stepped over to the bed. A book lay open on the night table, a novel. I recognized it from a series she'd read a few years ago. Maybe she was reading it again now, trying to recapture something from the time before everything changed.

I picked up the book. It smelled like pine trees and wintergreen and smoke. This was Jasey now. It smelled like Blake.

The walls closed in, clamping my ribs over my heart. I didn't want to know. It was like my lungs wouldn't take the air. I didn't want to know about Grandpa Jack, about Jasey's dad and my grandfather who lived in jail, about Jasey and Blake.

I put my hand on her shoulder and shook her.

"Jasey, wake up."

Her eyes opened, then widened in surprise. She sat up, looked around the room, then at her watch. "What are you doing here?"

I spoke before the words could stick in my throat.

"You're wasting yourself on Blake."

Jasey swung her legs onto the floor, yawned, and rubbed her eyes. "I don't need a lecture, Gavin." She yanked the book out of my hands and tossed it back on the table.

"Blake uses people, uses them up."

Jasey opened her mouth to interrupt but I kept going. "And those so-called friends of his, Clay and the others, they're using him. Blake's turning you into one of them."

She folded her arms over her chest. "You make it sound like I'm some kind of hostage. No one's taking anything from me that isn't freely given."

Bile climbed up my throat. I struggled to calm my voice. "Don't you see how bad he is?"

Jasey shrugged.

"He hurts people."

"He would never hurt me."

I sucked in a breath. I thought of the sound my mother's neck made when he shook her. "He will. Sooner or later."

She sighed. "Gavin, I think you're trying to look out for me, and that's sweet, but I don't need your protection. I'm just having some fun …"

"You're on a suicide mission," I interrupted. "Just like your father."

Her eyes flashed anger. "That is none of your business."

I barged on, my words angry too. "Because you think your father had what Grandpa Jack has, and that's why he killed himself. Because he was too afraid to live with it."

She raised her hand, and for a fractured instant I thought she was going to slap me. Her face twisted with such bitterness that I could have been looking at Blake.

"You don't know," I said. "You don't know if it was the disease that made him kill himself. You don't know if he even had it. Or that you'll get it."

She looked at me, her eyes hard, her lips clenched. "Like I said, this isn't any of your business. You have no idea what it's like to live with an inherited disease."

I wanted to put her hand on my nose so that she could feel the bone moving under the skin. I lifted a finger to my nose and softly tapped it. "Yes I do."

She studied me for a long time, the anger fading slowly from her eyes. "Okay. Maybe you do."

"Maybe your dad didn't have it, Jasey."

Her shoulders dropped in resignation. "Why else would he kill himself?"

I knew she was right. "But maybe you won't get it."

"Yeah. Like a reverse lottery. Maybe I won't die of a fried brain. But what about Trist? Even if I don't get it, what about him?"

I tried to sound calm despite the desperation I

was feeling. "Maybe he won't get it either."

"Everyone can't survive. Huntington's disease doesn't work that way. If Trist and I escape, Dad didn't. And neither did Grandpa Jack."

"You're giving in too soon, Jasey. You're acting like you're sure you're going to get it."

Her long silence closed around me like a cold rain. My words were barely more than a whisper. "You aren't, are you?"

She stood up then, crossing her arms. "Until I'm an adult, I can't get the test. Unless I show symptoms. And if there're already symptoms, what's the use of the test?"

She paced in front of the window, tugging her hands through her hair again and again.

"And is it such a good thing to know?" She paused at the window. "The test can only tell you that you've got the gene. It can't tell you when the symptoms will start. But if you know you're going to get it, isn't that almost the same as having it?"

If you know the beast is going to eat you, today or tomorrow or the day after that, no matter what you do, then how hard will you try to run away?

"Blake is just another kind of disease, Jasey. But at least for Blake, there's a cure."

Her eyes flashed, and she pointed to the door. "Then save yourself. I've got nothing to lose."

TWENTY-FIVE

[25]

I tossed my pack down on the grass and shoved open the door to the workshop. Grandpa Jack was standing at the bench, running a power sander over the wooden box he'd dug out of the trash bin.

My gaze traveled to his feet, laced into his sneakers, sure and still. Sometimes there was no sign at all of the disease. I pounded on the door so I wouldn't startle him. He looked up at me, his eyes crinkling into a smile under his safety goggles, and turned off the sander.

"It looks good," I said. The crate had a mellow golden sheen. "What kind of wood is it?"

"Maple, I think." He fingered the silky dust from the sander. "The hardest wood finishes the nicest."

I ran my hand over the box. It was smooth, warm from the sander. It felt like something alive.

"Trist is up in his room."

"I didn't come to see Trist." I didn't want to, either. What if he could see in my face what I knew about

Jasey and Blake? If he ever found out who Jasey was seeing, if any of the McVeighs did, I'd lose this family for sure. I toed the fine shadow of sander dust on the floor. "I was hoping you could help me with something."

"Maybe." He pushed the goggles up on his forehead.

I lead him out of the workshop to the back fence. I'd found my bike. It'd been tossed in the bottom of the gully where the high school kids like to party. Blake probably rode it there, then trashed it.

Grandpa Jack whistled. "That's a bit of a mess." He bent down to turn a pedal. It clacked on the frame. With one twist of his powerful shoulders the handlebars straightened, but the frame was still torqued. "Maybe if we heat it up." He wheeled the bike into the shop and stooped to take off the rims. "Why don't you loosen up the nut on the seat?" He whooped with laughter. "The nut on the seat. Get it?"

"Yeah. I get it. You're hilarious." I found a wrench on the workbench and removed the seat. Grandpa Jack upended the bike and clamped it on the bench.

I watched him working on the frame. He traced a torch over the metal, easing it back into shape. Sweat ran off his face and dark blotches soaked his shirt. He paused.

"You have any money for new rims? These ones are shot." He wiped his brow with his shirt sleeve.

"I'll have to save up for those. Maybe I can use the old ones for awhile?"

He shook his head. "No, they'll rub."

My face must have shown my disappointment, because he said, "I'll see if I can straighten them enough to use. No guarantees, though."

He turned off the torch and wiped his hands on a rag. "You've made some interesting discoveries lately."

My face flooded. "Discoveries?"

"About your brother."

"My brother?" I could feel my breath shortening into a pathetic wheeze.

He pulled off his goggles and wiped them clean with the rag. "Your nose. This bike."

"Oh, yeah." I sucked in a breath of relief. He wasn't talking about perfectly innocent, perfectly beautiful dark-haired girls.

He leaned back against the bench. "You can't always fix what's bent and broken. You can straighten it out, but there's going to be a twist left. A scar. I think your brother is like that. And I think you are too."

I'd wear the scar of my brother forever right in the middle of my face.

"I don't think much of Blake."

"No, I don't suppose you do."

"I don't think I'm like him." I couldn't keep the edge of anger from my voice.

"I'm not saying you act like Blake. But you are brothers. Nothing changes that."

He scratched his head and propped the goggles on his forehead. "Every family has its scars, Gavin. You take what you get. In this family it's the disease. Pat and I used to joke when we dropped a cup or misplaced our keys. 'It's the disease. It's going to get you.' When he started to shake, I wished it would get me instead."

My gaze dropped to the floor. I didn't want him looking at me, not now, reading my eyes, knowing what I knew.

"And sometimes," he held his hands in front of him, a barely perceptible shiver running through them, "sometimes I wonder if maybe it isn't done with this family."

He was studying his hands like they held the answer for him. How much longer until he too could see the beast?

He looked at me and grinned. "You're mighty serious all of a sudden. Never mind about the bike. We'll get it looking good again."

I wasn't worried about the bike. If anyone could fix it, it was Grandpa Jack. But I was hugely relieved to change the subject. "So, what are you going to do with this old box?"

"Couldn't tell you that. Not yet, anyway." He turned to the bench and unclamped my bike. "Funny, scars on old wood are a good thing. People will pay more for an old beat-up table than they will for a new one. They figure the dents and scratches give it character." He leaned the bike against the wall and turned back to me. "I've got a friend who makes stuff out of old barn wood—fancy shelves and cupboards. Sells them at boutiques. Old barn wood." He shook his head. "One man's garbage is another man's gold."

"Well, you'd know something about that." I made a point of looking at the sneakers on his feet, the ones he'd found in the trash. He followed my gaze.

"What's your size? I'll look for some for you too."

"No thanks. What if those were on a dead guy?"

"What, like I'm going to catch something from his shoes?"

"He could have died of athlete's foot. Or warts." Once I had a wart the size of a dime dug out from the bottom of my foot.

"No worries. I spray them with Lysol. And Raid." He laughed his booming laugh.

"I'll pass on the shoes. But thanks for fixing my bike."

"It isn't fixed yet. But leave it with me for a few days." He took a square of sandpaper and worked it into a corner of the box. "Sometimes you can fix something. Sometimes you can't." He puffed the dust off the box. It billowed and hung in the air like bits of a dream. He coughed, waving it away. "And sometimes there's an awful mess before you get it right."

Twenty-six

[26]

"No, Blake, I've already told you. I'm not giving you the money." Mom's voice was firm. "Even if I had it to give, and I don't, not with the dental work Gavin's going to need to fix the teeth you loosened."

I held my breath and listened at the kitchen door.

"If you need money so badly I suggest you find yourself a job."

I waited for the explosion. Nothing. Just silence. Then Blake, in a voice I hadn't heard him use in years. "I'll pay it all back."

Pleading. He was pleading. I wanted to burst out laughing.

"No." I heard pots and pans as she started supper.

"Please, Mom. You don't know how important this is."

"No."

This was so good. She wasn't angry. She wasn't scared. Mom was in control.

"Look, I've got myself in a bit of trouble. If you give me the money, I'll straighten out."

"No."

"It's trouble, Mom."

"I take it the leather jacket and all the new clothes weren't gifts?"

There was a pause, and even where I was standing I could hear him breathing. Don't push him too hard. He's on the brink.

"Just give me the money."

There was a sound of a pot lid coming down hard. "Blake, I'm not bailing you out of this one." Another pot.

"You're going to wake up Dad."

"I'm done talking about this."

"Then I guess you'll be spending that money on a funeral."

Silence. I could imagine her standing looking at him, a spoon poised in her hand. "What are you talking about?"

"I didn't mean to get in so deep. But I took money from the wrong people. That's why you have to give it to me." He paused. "You wouldn't want anything to happen to me, would you?"

Her voice was quiet. "No. I wouldn't."

Mom, don't give in now. Be strong. You can do it.

I heard her footsteps, then, "Make the call."

142

"Who do you think I'm going to phone, the police?"

"Yes. If you're in trouble with criminals, that's what you do."

"No." His voice was desperate. "I'd go to jail too. And there are others. Mom, I'm begging you, just give me the money."

There was a long pause, then, "I'd rather see you in jail."

A car pulled up to the house, Clay's car, I knew without looking. The engine revved and the windows rattled. Blake must have heard it too. The kitchen door flew open, just about flattening me against the house. He burst out, took one look at the car, and bolted in the other direction, disappearing into the darkness of the alley.

In the car a lighter flashed, and Clay's face was illuminated in glow. He was looking at me, the angles of his jaw sharp in the flare of the lighter. A red tip appeared. His cigarette. But he held the lighter for an instant more, and I read his face, the detachment, the menace.

The car crept away from the curb, its tail-lights snaking down the street. It circled and drove once more past the house, quiet, like a predator, then slipped into the night.

TWENTY-SEVEN

[27]

"There are others." I said the words softly to myself, Blake's words. Others, like Jasey. I smoothed the watercolor paper onto my school desk and taped the edges. With hands so used to the motion that it was almost unconscious, I sketched the trees around the boy's lake. Then I washed the background color, a hard steel gray, the color of a fall sky. The lake lay silver like the blade of a knife. The boy was going to die. There had already been snow. He was weak, thin, and by now, no one could even hope that he was still alive. On the shrubs in the undergrowth I dabbed bright red paint, not leaves, because these had already dropped, but berries—hard, inedible, bright red berries.

"There's another book, you know. About how he survives winter." Alexis was standing over my shoulder.

I drew the boy on his knees, either from weakness or in prayer.

"He lives like the Native people from a long time ago. It could be done."

I glanced up at her. Her brows framed her eyes, nice eyes, actually, a beautiful green flecked with gold. And long lashes. I felt myself redden and turned quickly back to the painting.

Troy appeared at my desk. "I got that book out now. It makes my feet sweat."

Roger looked up from his work. "It's a good book that makes your feet sweat."

Trist inspected the painting. "The guy looks different again."

"That doesn't matter," Alexis said. I was aware of her hand on the back of my chair. "The artist's perception of the character can change, just like the reader's." Her breath carried a faint whiff of peppermint.

Trist bent over the painting. "I know this guy." He tapped the paper with his finger as he thought. "He's someone I know."

Now my feet were sweating. "I don't think so, Trist. It's just a guy."

"No, it's not. It's a real person." He looked up at the ceiling, drumming his finger. "I know." He studied the figure. "I know who it is. It's your brother. It's Blake."

Alexis looked closely at the boy. "He's good looking."

Trist laughed mirthlessly. "You wouldn't want his brother Blake. No one in her right mind would. He's a psychopath."

My face was bright red by now. "I didn't mean him to look like anyone."

"See the way the hair kind of folds over his eyes, and the line of his jaw? That's him, all right!" Trist was jubilant in his discovery. "You painted your brother!"

Troy and Marc clustered around, passing their own judgment. "Yup, that's his brother. Should recognize the blood stains on his knee where he broke your nose."

"I'm surprised you didn't draw him like a dork."

"Or a pile of ..."

With one quick movement I tore the paper off the board and crumpled it, my desktop free of the images. Alexis gasped and the others fell quiet.

"I didn't mean for him to look like anyone. Okay?"

Trist crossed his arms and scowled. The others faded back.

"I'm just done painting. The kid's dead, or he should be by now. There's nothing more to paint."

The others went back to their desks, casting wary looks over their shoulders. I heaved the crumpled paper into the trash can and slumped in my chair. Trist came closer.

"I'm surprised you didn't paint him with horns

on his head," he hissed. "Especially knowing what you do."

I swiveled to look at him, my face flushing red. "What are you talking about?"

"Don't act more stupid than you really are. I can't believe it took you this long to find out. He's all but rubbed your nose in it."

"You mean Blake and Jasey, don't you?" I hated saying their names together. "How long have you known?"

He rolled his eyes. "Long enough."

"You should have told me."

He snorted. "What for? So you could jump into your superhero cape and save her? Or maybe you'd want to save your brother. But if you ask me, they're both such losers they make the perfect couple."

"Jasey's not like Blake."

"Oh, and I suppose you think she'd be better off with someone like you. Ha."

I felt the blood up around my ears again.

"I didn't say that …"

"Because I've seen how you look at her," he cut me off. "You're no different than your pig of a brother. Maybe worse. At least he doesn't pretend to be anything but scum."

I spun in my desk, away from him, blinking fast against his words.

He leaned across the aisle, his voice like acid in my ear. "Your old man, and that pathetic excuse of a mother, and Blake and you, you're all losers. And Jasey is too. I hope you're happy together."

It was no use trying to say something back. It would just sound lame. After a long time I felt Trist turn his glare away, and I let the drone of the classroom close around me.

The crumpled painting hung over the side of the trash can. Stupid kid. Just a hump of dead thing at the edge of the forest. The coyotes and bears would scatter his bones, birds would take his hair for their nests, pine cones would root in his compost, and as fast as he was there he'd be gone. He'd become the forest that swallowed him up in the first place. And no one would even know he'd been alive.

TWENTY-EIGHT
[28]

The kitchen was quiet when I got home. Mom was working most afternoons now, often into the evening. With a resigned sigh, I grabbed Bunny's lead from by the door and went to get her for her walk. A noise from the living room made me stop dead, the hairs lifting on my neck. I dropped the lead and peered around the corner into the gloom of the unlit room.

Blake was sitting in Dad's chair, his hands like claws on the arms, his face a ghostly white. He looked like a convict just before the executioner hits the juice to the electric chair. Something like a sob was leaking out of him.

I came around the corner and switched on the light.

"Turn that off!" He bolted from the chair and knocked my hand off the switch, plunging the room once again into a shadowless gray. Under his jacket his shirt was wet, like he'd been running. He smelled like the pig's-foot lamp. He smelled like fear. With a hateful look he slumped back into the chair.

"I should have knocked your teeth right out, then there'd be nothing to fix. Then the old lady would have given me the money." His nostrils flared like it was me who smelled bad. "Or I should have killed you. That would have solved all my problems."

"You make me sick." I turned to leave.

"When she comes home, she's going to give me the money."

I paused, his tone causing the old familiar fear to creep again around my heart. I turned to face him.

His eyes skated over my face. He looked sick, like a stray cat I saw once on our kitchen counter. It had torn open a hole in a bag of bread and was gulping down hunks while it watched me, not caring what I did to it because it was so close to death anyway.

His pasty face bent into an ugly grin. "I'm going to make her."

Blood throbbed in my temples as I struggled to calm my voice. "You're crazy."

"You're right."

The absolute coldness of his voice was terrifying.

"And Jasey's lost her mind to be with you."

"Jasey, Jasey, Jasey." He made a rude gesture with his tongue. "You know, she told me how you follow her around like a dog. Like she'd ever have anything to do with her pukey kid brother's ugly friend."

My head was hurting, and my arms and legs felt like the bones had been removed.

"You'll be lucky if you end up with someone called Tree Catcher." He flattened the end of his nose with his finger.

I let his insults land on me like punches, taking them with a kind of pleasure, almost, because the pain of his words reminded me I was still alive. And that his words were born of desperation.

"She loves me, Jasey does. She can't get enough of me." He got up from the chair, stumbling a bit. "And she'll do anything for me. So will the old lady. With the right kind of persuasion."

He shuffled to the back door. "She'll give me the money. All of it. And if she doesn't," he paused, yanking open the door, "then I'm going to kill her." The door clattered closed behind him.

I hardly hesitated in what I had to do. Like it was already decided. I eased my key into the deadbolt on Grandpa Jack's workshop, opened the door, and slipped inside.

Taking the flashlight from its bracket by the door, I shone a short beam onto the floor. The interior of the workshop appeared in muted yellow light. My bike, clamped on the workbench, sent a guilty shiver down my back. I slid open the third drawer of Grandpa Jack's tool chest and removed a set of small screwdrivers.

The doors on the Caddie were unlocked. I opened the driver's side and climbed in. The interior light illuminated the area under the dash. Working quickly, I removed the screws holding the disc player, eased the wires from their posts, and lowered the player onto the floor of the car. The half-dozen little screws left from the job lay like fallen guards on the carpet, and I screwed them back into their holes.

It wouldn't be enough. I knew that. But it would be a start. I put the tools and flashlight back, stole another quick glance at the bike, then left and closed the door.

With the player under my jacket, I went back home. I cracked open Blake's door and peered in to make sure he hadn't returned, then shoved into his room.

It stunk in there. My foot squished down on a wet towel. I flipped on the light and picked my way over dead laundry and food-encrusted plates to the bedside table. A half-drunk glass of milk, clotted in greasy white strands, teetered on the edge. Carefully, so as not to tip the glass, I picked up his phone and punched the first button on the speed-dial.

He answered on the second ring. "Clay." The sound of the car engine rumbled in the background. With appalling suddenness, my voice thinned to a whisper.

"Louder, you idiot."

I cleared my throat and the words barked out, "Clay, it's Gavin."

There was a long pause, and I wondered if maybe he hadn't heard me. Then, "What?"

"We need … I want … Can you come pick me up?" The phone slithered in my sweaty hands.

There was a short pause, then a snorting sound, then the phone went dead. I went outside to wait.

TWENTY-NINE

[29]

The metal of the disc player jabbed sharply into my side. I tugged my jacket more tightly closed, trying to erase the image of Grandpa Jack's face that lurked with me on the dark street. The drone of Clay's car grew steadily louder until it blatted up beside me at the curb. I slid into the front seat.

His pimpled profile didn't leave the road. He pulled away, accelerating at the corner onto the main road.

Again I cleared my throat. "Um. The reason I called ..."

His feral gaze met mine and the words were lost. I tried again. "I've decided, I mean, I wonder if you'll take me. Like a recruit. You know."

He laughed then, big snorting guffaws. "You?"

I pulled myself taller in the seat. "You said you saw potential in me. That I could work for you."

He laughed again. "Maybe so. But why now?"

"I want to work off Blake's debt." I pulled the

disc player from under my jacket and set it in my lap. "I brought this, and I'll do whatever you want."

Clay's mouth flattened into a frown. "You steal that?"

I nodded.

He cursed. "First off, you never, and I mean never, bring me stolen stuff. Pawn it, sell it, I don't care what you do with it, but I only want cash." His eyes turned back to the road. He fished out a cigarette from a pack on the dash, then flipped the pack to me.

With shaking fingers I pulled a cigarette from the pack. Clay held his lighter under my nose, and I tentatively puffed on the cigarette until a red glow appeared at the tip.

Immediately, tears squirted from the corners of my eyes as the searing smoke caught in my throat. I struggled against the impulse to cough, my face pounding red, until the pressure built so high that I had to, first a quiet bleat, then great ragged bursts.

A smirk played on Clay's face, but he didn't laugh. "Second, what's Blake's problem got to do with you?"

"He's my brother."

He laughed then, loudly. "Yeah. Lucky you." He eyed the long gray ash at the end of my cigarette. "Don't be dropping that on the floor." He motioned with his head toward the ashtray, and with an inexpert tap, I knocked off the ash. "But that doesn't tell me why you're here."

I shifted in the seat, trying to avoid the snake of smoke curling in front of me. "Well, it's just that he's kind of out of control."

"Uh-huh. So he threatened you to do this?" An edge of menace crept into Clay's voice.

"No," I replied quickly. "He doesn't even know."

Clay studied my face. "But he threatened somebody."

I swallowed foul-tasting spit. I would not admit the hold he had on my mother, and on Jasey. "It's not that."

Clay shook his head. "Let me tell you what Blake's real problem is. I could forgive him his debt, and have, really, even though he still owes me. Because there's no amount of money enough for what Blake has used in drugs. He's begged and stolen and you don't want to know what all, and he's still in so far that nothing you could do for him or me would be enough." He pulled deeply on the cigarette, letting the smoke escape around his teeth. "It's not about money, not anymore. It's about money for drugs, and that's an entirely different animal."

"But," the foul taste crept back up my throat, "what do I do?"

He eyed me briefly, one eyebrow lifting. He reached over to the disc player, popping open the disc drawer. He extracted the disc that had been left in there and held it up to read the title.

"Cowboy music?" He laughed softly. "Whoever you took this from needs it more badly than me." He tossed the disc into my lap. "Maybe you should take it back."

"I mean about Blake!" I slammed the disc back into the player. "Maybe you could talk to him. Maybe Jasey could. Maybe you could convince him to get into a program, or something."

Clay's jaw tightened. "First off, this isn't my problem. And it isn't yours, either. Second, Jasey's dumped him."

My mouth dropped open. "Jasey?"

He shrugged. "That shouldn't surprise you. I don't know what she was doing with him in the first place. And now he's a real load of laughs, shaking and sweating blood for his next fix."

I nodded dumbly.

He pulled up in front of the house. "Apparently Blake isn't too happy with Jasey right now. If I were you, I'd stay out of his way."

I stepped from the car, gratefully dropping the cigarette on the sidewalk and grinding it with my toe.

"Hey Gavin."

I looked back into his car.

"You're not really like him, you know. You have potential, all right. But all that's bent on you is your nose."

I would have said thanks, even though I wasn't sure he was really paying me a compliment, but I didn't say anything. I felt it at first rather than heard it, that sound coming from our house. But then I did hear it, and it stopped my heart.

"No, Blake! Please!"

Clay was looking toward the house, his eyebrows knotted. "Is that your mom?"

I couldn't answer him because I was already running, couldn't answer because of the scream building in my own throat.

THIRTY

[30]

Black lake water. The night closed over me as I ran to the house. I could hear Blake shouting, his words an indiscriminate roar, and Mom's screams, like metal rasps that tore at the night.

I could feel screams in my own throat, airless screams like in a dream. But this was no dream. Blake had Mom.

I cursed my stodgy legs, willing more strength to my feet, needing to be there and never getting there, and the screams were louder now.

Please God …

The steps were like a rock wall and I stumbled, a numbing pain gripping my knee. I scrabbled at the handle, fumbling, my hands suddenly like mittens.

"I'll get it, Gavin."

Jasey reached from behind me and turned the handle.

Breathless, I stammered, "What …?"

"Clay phoned me. Trist is calling the police. Right now. Come on."

I shook my head. "No. You can't go in there. Just go home." I pushed her hand away from the door.

She put her hand over mine and held it. "I can talk to him."

"No." I was desperate to get in, and desperate to make her go away. "You don't know what he's doing. What he's going to do."

Her gaze fell to my nose. "Oh, I think I do."

There was no fear in her eyes, and that's what frightened me the most. It was like she wanted to go in. She wanted to face that beast.

"No."

She shouldered her way past me into the house.

"No!"

But the sound disappeared in the anguished cry of my mother. "Blake, please!"

I bolted into the house behind her.

Every cupboard door in the kitchen was open, the stuff in heaps on the counter and floor. The drawers were yanked out and upended. The fridge door swung back and forth, a jug of milk on its side dribbling into a white pool on the floor.

Mom's voice came from the living room. "Don't. Please don't!"

I clawed at Jasey, but she pulled away.

Please, please God …

Mom was on the floor in the living room, a trickle of blood from one nostril running down over her mouth. She was holding her right arm close to her chest. When she saw me, she started to cry.

Dad was standing at the edge of the room in his T-shirt and underwear. Sweat was beading on his forehead, and his eyes were round with fear.

Bunny was at his feet, a low growl rumbling from her throat.

Blake's back was to us. He turned, slowly, and when he saw Jasey, his eyebrows lifted briefly, then snagged again into a vicious knot.

"Well, look who's come crawling back."

He continued to turn, the ugliness in his face like dark stripes on his glue-white skin. He was trembling.

"And with my useless brother."

If I were drawing Blake right then, he'd have spirals in his eyes. I opened my mouth to speak, then I saw it, and I struggled to find spit to swallow.

He was gripping Dad's gun.

"Come on, Blake." Jasey's voice was calm, placating. "You don't want to be doing this."

He spat a curse at her.

Dad took a step toward him, and Blake spun, the gun at the end of his arm aimed at Dad's head. Mom gasped. Dad froze.

"Give me the gun." Jasey extended her hand. "Then we can walk for awhile. Talk things out."

He laughed, phlegm rattling in his throat. "Like I am so stupid," he sneered.

"No, really. I've been thinking. We should talk. I didn't mean what I said."

A flash of hope crossed Blake's eyes, and I almost felt sorry for him. I think I could understand how he loved Jasey McVeigh. But Blake's face hardened, and he scowled.

"You're lying." And he swung the gun toward her.

THIRTY-ONE
[31]

It's funny what you remember. I remember how the pig's-foot lamp shattered with the blast of the gun. And how the cat rocketed out from under the couch. And the feeling in my ears, like a pencil eraser was being driven into my eardrums.

I ducked instinctively. Jasey brought her arm up in front of her face. Shards of wood and pig foot and broken light bulb drilled into the wall.

Dad dove in front of Mom to shield her. I could hear her sobbing, and Dad telling her to keep her head down.

Blake's arm windmilled with the recoil of the gun, his eyes frightened now, and wild. He aimed the gun again.

I shouted, or I tried to. There was an iron collar around my neck. "Jasey!"

She looked, I know she did. She saw him aiming the gun at her. But she stood like she hadn't heard me. She squared her shoulders, and I saw her take a big breath. And she just stood there.

She was waiting to die.

Dad was clambering to his feet, his chest heaving with horror.

A siren, far away, started to wail.

I moved, but maybe it was just in my mind, because in my imagination I threw myself in front of Jasey, taking the bullet instead of her. Taking it right in the heart. But if I did move, it wasn't fast enough. I saw Blake's finger close on the trigger at the same time I heard my father.

"Sic 'im!"

Bunny streaked in front of me, leaping, her jaws agape, focused on Blake's extended arm.

The room rocked with the gun blast and the hollow thud of the bullet as it entered Bunny's body. The dog's head snapped back, then dropped forward as she fell, her eyes still open.

Jasey lowered her arm, her eyes registering surprise at the dead dog in front of her. She blinked, and her eyes grew wide. It was like she was waking up. She started to shake.

Blake laughed, a hysterical laugh. He looked at the dog, then at Jasey, then at the rest of us. He laughed again, once, more uncertain, and his whole body shook.

There were many sirens now, and closer.

Dad took a careful step toward him.

Jasey dropped her arms to her sides.

Mom curled up on the floor, her knees drawn up to her chest.

And again, Blake lifted the gun.

My leaden feet refused to move, but I reached with my arm for Jasey, reached to pull her from the bullet's path. But she moved too, in long strides, right toward Blake.

He had placed the gun against his temple.

"Blaaaaake!" Jasey dove for him.

Sirens punctured the night and their lights cut red and blue swaths over the living room walls.

She was still crying his name when the shot exploded, still crying as they fell to the floor, still crying as she rolled off him, her shirt red with his blood.

The sudden silence hammered around my head and I crumpled to the floor. I crawled toward them.

I heard Dad calling to the police, "An ambulance! We need an ambulance!"

Mom was so pale her skin looked like skimmed milk. She was struggling to get to her feet, holding her arm. I could see a knob on her upper arm where a broken bone protruded.

Blake was on his back. A small hole pegged through his jacket. His eyes were closed, his breath in bubbles clinging to blue lips.

"Oh God."

I looked up to see Dad, his eyes rimmed with red, his hands trembling. He knelt down beside me.

Police officers jammed into the room. More sirens screamed outside

"We're going to need some room." An officer rested his hand on my shoulder.

"Oh God." A sob caught in my father's throat.

An ambulance attendant helped Jasey up, wrapped a blanket around her shoulders, and led her away.

The officer's hand on my shoulder tightened. "C'mon, son. You'll have to move from the scene."

I shrugged from beneath his grip. An attendant handed Dad a blanket.

At first I thought he was going to cover Blake's face. I wanted to cry out, "No, he's not dead. See, he's breathing."

But Dad put the blanket around me. I stumbled to my feet, suddenly aware that my pants were wet. I started to cry.

Dad wrapped me in the blanket, enclosing me in its warmth. He took me gently by the arms and pulled me into him. He held me against his chest and rested his cheek against my head. I could feel him crying, I knew he was, and I let him hold me like that. Even as his tears ran down into mine.

THIRTY-TWO

"It won't be the same." Grandpa Jack ran a soft cloth over my bike, then wheeled it toward the door. "But it'll work just fine. Once you get new rims you won't notice any vibration. And I hope you like the color." He laughed. "I was all out of deck paint."

He'd matched the silver paint exactly.

"It looks great. Thank you, Grandpa Jack."

He rubbed my shoulder and grinned. "You'll pay me back."

A shudder of conscience rippled my skin. I'd brought him back the disc player. When he'd taken it from me, he'd said, "Blake?" Then he'd inspected the neatly disengaged wires, looked at me hard, and said, "I thought I'd left the door unlocked."

I wheeled the bike out of the workshop and set it on its stand. The sun caught the silver paint and reflected it in hundreds of tiny rainbows.

"You coming in?" Grandpa Jack held the back

door open. Through the doorway I could see Trist, watching us.

"Maybe for a minute. I was going to go up to the hospital."

"Any progress?"

"Some. He's sitting up now."

Grandpa Jack nodded. "It'll take some time."

"Yeah."

Troy and Marc figured I should be throwing a party because Blake was partially paralyzed. Alexis didn't say much, but she didn't have to. Her eyes told me that she knew what I was feeling. When Charlie Able joked about rehabs and made his wrists all crooked and gimpy, she punched him so hard that he had to run to the washroom so no one would see him cry.

Grandpa Jack settled onto his chair and picked up the newspaper. Behind him, Trist watched his grandfather's feet as they broke into their familiar dance.

Trist lifted his chin, his eyes on the ceiling. He blinked, and bit his lip.

The anger was gone from him, but I'd have the anger over the loss I read now in his face.

Grandpa Jack looked up from his paper. "You'll come on Friday then, for Monopoly?"

"Yeah. I'd like to."

Trist nodded at me, and a weak smile broke on his face. "Prepare to be whipped."

The door to Blake's hospital room opened and Jasey slipped into the corridor. She started when she saw me. "Oh, Gavin. I was just leaving."

"Uh-huh." I dropped my gaze to the checked tile floor.

"I was just keeping him company. And I gave him the ring back."

I looked up at her. "How did he take that?"

She shrugged. "I think he understands."

I breathed again, relieved. "So, you're okay?"

"Better than I was. Trist and I are seeing a woman at the home where Uncle Pat stays. Mom got us hooked up. She counsels people who are at risk of Huntington's disease."

"Trist too?" I couldn't keep the surprise from my voice.

She nodded. "I think he's known as long as I have. Maybe longer. He just didn't want to know."

"But no one else?"

"No. Not yet."

Her face brightened. "You know what Grandpa Jack did? He made a chest for me out of an old box.

It's beautiful, all varnished and shining. It's for holding treasures."

"Like a hope chest."

"I guess." She glanced over her shoulder at Blake's room. "I hope he's okay."

He'll never walk, and he'll be lucky to recover the use of his arms so that he can push a wheelchair. "Me too."

"I should go." She looked embarrassed all of a sudden.

"It's okay," I blurted. "What you did. You saved him."

"I think some people would say it would have been better if he'd died."

"He's got another chance now, Jasey."

She took a big breath and her words came out like a sigh. "In a weird way, I think he saved me. Even before all this happened." She motioned to the hospital room. "His sickness with the drugs ... I could see how it was changing him. He made me see how much a day matters when it's all you've got left."

"Then I'm glad."

She lifted her hand to my cheek. "You've got today too."

I blushed bright red. "Maybe I should go in. Mom just dropped me off on her way to work. And Dad will be here in a while."

She nodded, and for an instant I thought she was going to cry. But then she smiled and dropped her hand. "So, I'll be seeing you."

"Yeah." I pushed open the door to Blake's room.

"Gavin?"

I turned.

"Thanks."

She took a step away from me, then lightly she turned and walked down the hall.

Blake was propped in a wheelchair by the window, his head supported with rolled towels, a blanket tucked around his legs. A potted plant by his bed leaned happily to the sunlight. Get-well cards were taped up on the wall so he could see them. Ms. Priestly had sent him one. So had Mr. Murphy. He'd wanted to give him a puppy, but Dad had said maybe when he came home. On a small table by Blake's chair was a cup with a straw, and beside it, Jasey's emerald ring.

I didn't want to stare at it but it hypnotized me, lying there all gold and green on the woodgrain tabletop. Blake followed my gaze.

"It's a nice ring. You should give it to Mom," I said.

His eyes tracked my face for a long time. I hoisted myself up on the windowsill and pulled a novel out of my jacket pocket.

Several floors below me, the parking lot buzzed with cars and people. Grandpa Jack's old Caddie eased up to the curb by the main entrance. Jasey's slim figure came out onto the sidewalk, the sun dancing on her dark curls.

Grandpa Jack got out of the car and handed Jasey the keys. He slid into the passenger seat while Jasey got in behind the wheel.

The car took to the main street in an exuberant cloud of exhaust. I watched it until I couldn't see it anymore, then turned again to Blake.

"You remember what happened last time? The plane goes down in the middle of nowhere and the kid survives?" I flipped open the book to where we'd left off. I cleared my throat, then in a clear strong voice Ms. Priestly would have loved, I started to read.